MW01656940

This book is dedicated to my Brother Shane who is in Heaven.

Anna, ~~I~~ hope you like the book.

Travis

Chapter One

Shane

March, 8th 2:00 A.M. 2019, near Lake Mead

I lay near my car all bloody and unable to move, a few feet away from the Toyota rental, both my wife and son was still inside. I could feel that my ribs were broken with my left leg and arm was useless after flying out the car and into some rocky formation. I used my right arm to pull myself towards the car that was flipped over onto its roof. I could see Tristan in the backseat and Christine was inside the vehicle not moving and bloody. It was raining so it helped me stay alert somewhat as I got closer. On the broken guard rail, I could see a man standing near it with a flashlight pointing it at me.

“Sir!! Don’t move around! I have emergency services coming!” He yelled.

I finally got to the open door of the Toyota. “Christine! Are you ok honey? Tristan, can you hear me?’

I could see that blood was seeping from my wife’s face and a shard from the windshield had entered her neck. Tears flowed from my eyes looking at her and then at Tristan, he was buckled in but not moving. I took my right hand to shake him awake.

“Tristan?” I said weakly.

I could tell his neck had snapped from the impact of the crash, I pushed myself back over near Christine so I could touch her face and lay next to her. This was all my fault I realized; I should have waited until daylight for the long drive from Las Vegas to the Grand Canyon but I was excited to go after a big victory in the boxing ring. Five hours earlier, I was getting ready for the biggest fight of my life and pay day I have ever won. I also was scheduled to be shown on primetime tv with this fight. My name is Shane “Lightning Fists” Avis, I was a contender for the middle weight championship, I am 5'7 and 160 pounds of muscle, shaved head and Goatee so not a bad looking guy. My wife Christine, had dirty blond hair and was beautiful, that kept herself in shape from marathon running. Tristan was an energetic little blond boy of 6 years of age that was autistic but very artistic if he had lived, he would have been an artist. I could feel the life leaving me as blood drained from my side, which had a gash ten inches long. I tried to stay close to Christine as I felt I was close to dying.

"I'm sorry baby, I'm sorry," I whispered.

I could hear the sirens getting close as I began to close my eyes and dream of me being back in the MGM Grand casino in Vegas getting ready for my fight. I was in the locker room where we were getting ready. I was in front of a mirror, shadow boxing with my trainer, Vinny DeLuca behind me talking encouraging words. I was wearing blue trunks with a Lightning stripe on the side of them with some Nike shoes.

"That's it, Shane, your looking good there," Vinny said. "Your opponent won't know what hit him."

Out of the corner of my eye, I saw my father walk into the locker room with my mother and my wife. Christine looked gorgeous in her black sexy dress, blond hair done up and long luscious legs walking in high heels. I stopped shadow boxing and turned to Vinny.

"Hey, give me a few minutes with the folks and my wife," I said.

My father was 6'0 ft. and in ok shape for a guy in his 70's, he wore a black Brooke Brothers suit since he is a real estate agent with the handsome look, grey hair and goatee. My Mother wore a light blue and flower sun dress since it is warm in Las Vegas. I stepped over towards the door to the locker and could hear the crowd getting excited for the other fight that was already coming to an end.

"Coming to wish me luck?" I asked.

My father smiled." As matter a fact we are, I was wondering if you were having an after party once you win?"

"I promised Christine, I would take them to the Grand Canyon after the fight," I said as I put my arm around Christine's waist.

She kissed my cheek affectionately." We both thought while we were in Vegas, we would take Tristan there to see the sights since our hometown is Duluth, MN."

"Well, beware there might be a storm later tonight so drive careful," My father said.

"I will pop thanks," I said.

I could see Vinny talk to a security guard at the door then he walked over to where we were standing.

"They're ready for you Shane, we are up next," Vinny said.

I gave a hard long kiss to Christine." Alright, babe head back to the seating arrangements, I'll win this quick. Mom and Dad, talk to you in a little while."

They headed out the door as my promoter and manager, DeMarcus Bell stepped in the doorway wearing an Everlast shirt with a Lightning fists logo on it. He was tall at 6'4 ft and had a basketball figure on him and dark skinned.

He smiled wide." You ready for the big-time baby! This is it; you get this win we will have a shot at the title in 2 months' time. Let's get out there."

Evan Abrams was carrying his doctor's bag with tools to stop the cuts; he was my cut man and physician even though he was still a few months from getting his license. He was a young Jewish guy at my height and was a nice guy, he also wore the Everlast shirt with my logo. We headed out the door with my crew behind me as the crowd went wild in the stadium as we walked towards the boxing ring. The place was packed as we ushered in by security and my crew to the ring. I could see the ring announcer standing in the middle of the ring waiting for the microphone to lower down from the ceiling. I got into the ring and did a little dance with the flash of my fists to impress the crowd. They roared approval as my opponent started walking down from an opening on the opposite side of the building. He seemed to be more muscled and taller than me, I knew this was going to be a tougher fight for me. My father and mother, along with my wife sat near my corner. I had given them a quick wave before stepping through the ropes and showing off. I looked over at my opponent that was contender for the middle weight championship. His name was Reilly "The Irish Bull" McDonough, he was about six feet tall with an athletic build, wearing the Irish flag for shorts and gloves. Even his robes were basically the Irish flag with the Irish bull logo on back of it. The ring announcer grabbed the microphone and turned towards me and pointed.

"In this corner! Is Shane the lightning fists Avis!! A record of 20-1 with 20 knockouts!" The ring announcer said in his best Michael Buffer impersonation.

He turned to Reilly and pointed at him. "In this corner is Reilly the Irish bull McDonough!! Former champion and with a record of 35 and 2 losses! With 20 knockouts!! The fight will go eight rounds. Let's get ready to rumble!!"

The crowd roared as certainly he was the favorite to win but I was going to prove them wrong. The referee signaled for us to get in the middle of the ring so both crews moved to the middle, where I began a deadpan stare at Reilly.

"No below the belt shots and let's have a clean fight, touch gloves! "The referee said loudly.

Reilly smashed my gloves down then backed away to his corner to wait for the bell to sound and the chaos to begin. While I was waiting for the bell to sound, Vinny called out to me.

"Remember to keep your distance and use the jab to start off!!" Vinny yelled.

I nodded as the bell sounded and began circling with Reilly, trying to keep my distance from his fists. I caught him with the jab then evade a few of his shots and pop-pop with the jab for the whole round. Evan began cleaning my face then gave me some water and a spit bucket while Vinny spoke.

"Alright Kid, not too bad out there, now add a hook or uppercut with the jab, overtime it's going to slow him down," Vinny said then the referee motioned end of break.

I sat up and they took the stool away when the bell sounded and we began our war dance all over again. He started getting through my defense a little and getting punch in, hitting my left eye. I would counter with some jabs and a right hook, plus getting to Reilly's midsection with a few blows. This went on for some time like this until the end of the sixth round, he was able to get a powerful uppercut to my jaw. I saw stars, once he connected with a hook and I sat down on the boxing ring floor against the ropes as the referee got in front of me and began the count.

"One! Two!" He yelled.

"Get up Shane! Move damnit!" Vinny screamed. "Beat the 10 count!"

I shook my dazed head as I begum climbing up the ropes, pulling myself up by the count of 8 getting angry at myself.

The referee put 2 fingers in front of my face." You good? You alright to continue on?"

I nodded as he stepped back to get the middle of ring, then he signaled for the fight to continue. He came rushing at me, trying to finish me off but I responded back with a series of Jabs and a hard right hook that began to daze Reilly. I took advantage of an opening and got a hard uppercut in with the hard right hook that made Reilly fall against the ropes before the bell sounded. I went back to my corner and Evan came out and began treating a cut to my right eye as Vinny yelled at me.

"Kid, you were just lucky you beat the 10 count from the referee," Vinny said." No more games out there, you take him down this round, he's tired and hurt from the last blows you landed. You take him out!"

I nodded as he pushed the mouth piece back in my mouth and I stood up for the bell to sound again for the fight to start.

It was round seven and I was stilled pissed off I went down from an uppercut so when the bell sounded, I started my little war dance, hitting with jabs and the right hook. Vinny was right, the Irish bull was running out of the gas and was feeling all the blows I was giving him. It was near the end of the seventh round when I found the opening for a powerful uppercut and hard right hook to the head. My fists started to go at lightning speed with nonstop hooks which sent Reilly to the boxing mat. The referee began the ten count and everything felt like slow motion as Reilly tried grabbing to pull himself up the ropes to stand. The referee screamed ten but he was just on his knees. I raised my arms in victory and ran back to Vinny, my whole crew lifted me up for a few minutes the dropped me back down.

"Great job kid!" Vinny said.

Evan began taking off my gloves while the physicians tended to Reilly and getting coherent so the judges could give their final decision. I went over to Reilly's corner.

"Good fight out their man, I'm sorry I had to knock you down and God bless," I said.

Reilly nodded and grabbed my hand, shaking it. "The better man won, I hope you get a title shot and good luck."

I nodded then got to the middle of the ring with my crew and waited for the ring announcer to let the crowd know of the decision. The ring announcer took my arm and raised it.

"Winner by Knockout, Shane' Lightning Fists" Avis!!!!" The ring announcer yelling into the Microphone.

The crowd went wild, clapping and screaming, I felt great and the rest of the time was a blur until we got in and began driving the long trek to the Grand Canyon. It was dark and began raining hard. Christine and Tristan were both resting while I drove and that's when it happened, a semi-truck was coming around a curve but too far out. It connected with the front, crumpling it and put us into the guard rail. We flipped over and over, my door flew open and I ripped out of my seat belt, landing into a rocky hillside, I could feel my legs, ribs and my left arm bent into an odd position. I was out for a good 5 minutes that's when I woke in lots of pain and seeing the destruction of the car. I had heard the man scream down but concentrated on pulling myself to the car and check on Tristan and Christine. I laid next to Christine and just waited for my end so I could be with them. Five months prior, my younger brother Trey had committed suicide because of a devastating divorce that put his business into ruin. While I was bleeding out, I could see him with a cigarette in his hand smoking next to me. He had been about the same height and a little heavier with darker brown curly hair that was short, glasses, moustache. He always wore jeans, t-shirt and his Vikings football jacket. Once I saw him looking at me, I knew it would be the end for me. He just stood next to me, not saying a word. The sirens were really loud and I could hear men scrambling to the vehicle as I let the darkness take me.

Chapter Two

April 15th, 2019. Summerlin Hospital, Las Vegas 8:00 am

I awoke very confused and weak. I could feel tubes coming out of my body and I could barely move. It was a hospital that I could tell with a drape blocking my view of an exit while nurses and doctors walked the hallways. I knew I must be at the intensive care somewhere; my only right arm could move. I could tell my head was stationary by some device, my left arm and leg in a cast and my right foot was inside some type of block, holding it straight. I turned my head to the left slightly and could see Trey sitting next to me smoking a cigarette. It seemed strange to me since it was a hospital and he was dead. It could be I was dead and in an Autopsy room? I really didn't know. The smell of the cigarette seemed strange but I really didn't know if I was really in a hospital or not. Until someone opened the curtain, she was a tall woman with glasses, older about 50 with a bright smile on her face.

"Well, I am so glad your awake Mr. Avis. You put a scare in all of us," she said. "The doctor will be becoming around shortly to speak to you.

All I could do is groan and moan since I could feel tubes coming out of my throat, plus I wore a neck brace to keep my head steady. She closed the hospital curtain again. Trey had disappeared from his sitting position and I felt alone, I began wondering where Tristan and Christine were. I must have been there for hours, when a nurse had to come in with a catheter to relieve me. It was quite painful and then a little while a doctor showed up. He was average height and a little on the heavy side with glasses and balding. He smiled down at me.

"Mr. Avis, I am glad to see your awake," he said. "I am Doctor Hostetler, the surgeon who worked on you while you were in a coma. Tomorrow morning, I will be coming down to take the tracheal tube out of your throat so you can eat regularly and talk. I will go over a plan to get you back up and walking again with some physical therapists. Have a good day Mr. Avis."

All I could do was nod before he walked away from me. A nurse stopped by and put the tv on for me so I could watch some boxing. That's when I saw the news on TV, it said I was finally out of a coma after a tragic accident that killed my wife and child. All I could do was cry and wonder why God let me live, if he was punishing me. I felt so weak and knew I damn well wasn't 160 pounds anymore. The tomorrow seemed like forever to get there, especially when they wake you up to empty your bladder with a catheter. It was about nine in the morning before the doctor showed up with a young male assistant with him both in white medical coats. He leaned down with a flashlight checking my throat for a few moments then looked at me.

"OK, Mr. Avis we will be taking out the tube and try to be quick about it," he said. "We can't use any anesthesia so it will hurt for a few moments."

The young man had some bandages near him and antiseptic wipes close by my bed once the doctor leaned over me. I closed my eyes and braced for the pain as he began pulling the tracheal tube out of my throat. Tears streamed out of my closed lids, even if it happened in 10 seconds. After he took it out, the assistant cleaned around the wound and bandaged my throat, it felt a lot better. I opened my eyes and the assistant gave me drink of water with a straw sticking out of the cup.

"Just make sure when you talk, hold onto the gauze, it will keep the hole in your throat closed so you can speak clearly," Doctor Hostetler said. "I will contact your parents and trainer to tell them you will be ready for visitors. You will be moving to a normal room today."

I nodded then held the gauze. "Thank you doctor."

The two doctors left me and it was a couple of hours more when 2 nurses came and unhooked stuff from the medical bed then wheeled me out through a maze of hallways. We went in an elevator and stopped on floor 5. They pushed me past a nurse's station, where I got looks of curiosity as they wheeled me by. They put me in a spot where the window was and the view of the parking lot. I asked the one of the nurses to turn the tv on and them find me ESPN so I could watch some golf. I looked at my watch and it was lunchtime on Tuesday, I could hear my belly actually growl. A female nurse entered the room with a lunch tray, she was about 5'5 and slightly heavier looking with big breasts, probably 40 D cup size, big hips and buttocks. She had the most angelic face I have seen on a woman though with black rimmed glasses and long wavy brunette hair. She sat down next to me and I could smell a lavender perfume of some sort. She was wearing purple scrubs and Tennis shoes.

"I'm Courtney Ray, Mr. Avis, I will be your nurse's aide for 2 days a week," Courtney said in a slight southern drawl. "I will be helping you out for a few hours a day with cleanliness and lunch of course.

"It's nice to meet you Courtney, I'm Shane," I said holding the gauze. "t's a pleasure to meet you. What's on the menu?"

She smiled then took the top off the tray." Mashed potatoes with meat gravy and for dessert is red Jell-O. A meal fit for a king."

I tried not to laugh but smiled wide. "I am sure it is, could you angle it for my good arm."

She put it next to my good arm and placed it close to me. She then looked at the doctor's chart then back at me as I ate the mashed potatoes.

"It says here in 1 week your left arm and leg cast will be removed so you can start working on getting out of this hospital," she said.

"That's good news, maybe in a couple of months I will be able to start training for boxing again," I said.

She looked at me very interested. "You're a boxer? I used to go to the fights with my father when I was a little girl in Iowa."

"Well, if we ever can get some boxing on ESPN here would you mind watching it with me?" I asked.

She nodded as she helped wipe my face, her lavender was slightly intoxicating and made me ashamed that I was slightly aroused by her. Especially, after my wife and child dying in some car accident I caused. I looked at her.

"I know this is a strange thing to ask since this is not a hotel but do they have a bible here?" I asked.

She smiled. "If I cannot find one Shane, I will bring one of my own for you."

I finished my mashed potatoes and started nibbling on the Jell-O.

"So do you work somewhere else also, Courtney?" I asked.

"I work as a Home Health Aide on the weekends so I can basically have full time to make it," Courtney said.

I felt a little red when I asked." Are you married Courtney? Have kids?"

"I have one girl, aged 6 and no Shane, I am not married, the guy I was with passed away of an overdose of Meth 2 years ago," Courtney said.

My eyes began tearing." I'm sorry Courtney, that must be painful. Both my wife and child are gone also. Tristan would have been 7 this year."

She rubbed my arm lightly. "I'm sorry too Shane. God will guide us through this hard time for you or I will."

I finished my Jell-O and she set the plate on her little lunch cart. “Do you need anything else before I have to go serve some other people?”

“The company you work for so when I get out of here, I can get some help,” I said. “Maybe a business card if that’s not too forward.”

She smiled and actually took a card from her front pants pocket that she handed me, which had her number on it and health aide company she worked for.

“There you go Shane, it was very nice meeting you and I will see you tomorrow,” Courtney said.

She wheeled out the cart and headed down the hallway and I was again left alone for a while just watching a strongman competition on ESPN. I was of course interrupted by a nurse to empty my bladder again with a catheter. I really hoped the doctor would prescribe me a med to get my bladder working right so I could stop getting the punishment. After she was done, Vinny walked through the door, carrying some boxing and wrestling magazines in his hands. He set them on a portable tray holder next to my bed.

“Champ! I am so glad your awake!” Vinny said. “I was really worried about you but they wouldn’t let me see you until you got out of ICU.”

“How’s Evan doing?” I asked.

“Evan finally got his license to become a doctor but he is still working for me,” Vinny said.

I smiled and nodded, then Doctor Hostetler walked in with clipboard in hand in his white medical coat.

“Well, it’s nice to finally meet the great Vinny DeLuca, they got you up there with Kevin Rooney and Angelo Dundee as the greatest trainer,” he said. “I’m sure Shane will need some training again in coming months to get back in form.”

Vinny looked me over." When will Shane get the neck brace off Doc and the casts?"

"He had some trauma from the car accident with the broken bones and whiplash, it will come off next week with all the casts, "Hostetler said.

Vinny nodded. "Once he gets himself up and at least walking then we will start working again."

"That sounds good, I am not going to tell Shane there's no doubt he will never fight again since the human body is a remarkable thing," Hostetler said. "Shane, I prescribed you a med to help and hopefully get your bladder back to normal."

I nodded as he put a piece of paper on the portable tray next to my bed.

"Also, next Tuesday your casts come off and I will enroll you in the recovery center next door to the hospital," he said. "You will be probably in their for five weeks before letting you go home."

I nodded. "I figured that since I can barely move now. Has my father come by yet?"

Hostetler shook his head. "He came once after he knew you were out of danger. I expect since I called him to let him know you were out of the coma; he will drop by."

"Listen kid, I will go call your pops again to see when he will drop by," Vinny said. "Going to find cafeteria to grab some to eat then be back up."

I waved with my good arm as he headed out the door. Hostetler sat down in the chair next to the bed.

"Mr. Avis, I am not going to lie, this will be a long recovery so you will be out of the fight game and work in general," Hostetler said. "You have a plan to stay afloat? An administrator will be up to work on papers so you can either get medical assistance to pay the bill."

I nodded. "That's why I was hoping my dad stopped by since he has all of my medical insurance information. I know there is a chance I may not be able to fight but I at least want to be able to work somewhere or be mobile enough to do it."

Hostetler patted my arm. "I think anyone with a passion to get out of the hospital will at least get mobile, Shane. Alright, some physical therapists will be starting next week to work on leg strength to get you walking."

He stood up and headed for the door as Vinny walked in with a cup of coffee in his hand, sipping at it. They nodded to each other as they passed each other and Vinny took a seat next to my bed again.

"So, they going to get all the casts off next week?" Vinny asked. "Then you can start getting to work and getting out of here."

I nodded. "I will be ecstatic once that happens then it will be in no time I will be getting out of here."

"I let your dad know you need him here to get the financial stuff done here so you can be able to get the hospital bill paid," Vinny said. "He said he would stop by tomorrow and get things done."

I felt a little more relaxed once he said that. "Glad to hear it, I know the bill is going to be huge after being in a coma for a month and getting patched up."

'I did get your cellphone from the police the other day," Vinny said. "From the wreckage of the car."

He set the cracked Apple iPhone on the portable tray then his phone rang which Vinny answered.

"Got to take this call Shane," he said.

I nodded as he hurried out of the hospital room and I was left alone with the tv going, so of course I watched more ESPN. About twenty minutes later, Vinny was coming back into the room with Evan in tow. He was all smiles and it made me glad I at least had these guys as friends and co-workers. I'm sure Vinny was promoting and coaching another fighter who could be fighting in Vegas but at least they remembered to visit.

"Evan, so glad you could make it! I've missed that smiling face," I said. "Does DeMarcus have a fight in Vegas then?"

"Yeah, he does, he's just too lazy to stop to see his second-best fighter start recuperating from near death," Evan said." I swear that guy is an A-Hole. How you holding up Shane?'

"Good, I am just glad now I am getting to eat food and not be on a feeding tube anymore," I said. "And actually, getting to talk to people without tubes down my throat."

Evan smiled." I understand, I'm just glad you're still alive Shane, that car accident looked bad,"

Vinny patted my arm. "We have one more day in town so we will come back and visit again. Darius Williams is the one fighting tonight. If he wins, he will be contender for the Light heavyweight Championship."

My eyes widened. "Wow, give Darius my best, will he be on ESPN tonight?"

Vinny nodded. "Should be a hot fight, he will be facing a Russian named Vladimir Chatzky, the Russian beast. He looks a little tougher than Darius but he's a good outside fighter."

I nodded my head. "I have sparred with him once or twice; I can tell he is pretty great. Made me tougher for my fights."

Evan set some more boxing and MMA magazines on the portable tray next to my bed.

"I hope this will keep you occupied for at least a bit, "Evan said. "Until you start get moving and working on lots of therapy."

"The doctor is setting it all up, by next week, all the casts will come off and I can start working to get my body moving again," I said.

"The fight will be on at or after nine PM tonight on ESPN, I hope you get to watch it," Vinny said. "If I can get DeMarcus off his ass to visit before he leaves, I will make sure he does."

Both the physician and trainer gave me a hug then walked out of the room and I got stuck looking out the window at the cars parking in the hospital lot. Vinny had left my cellphone and charger on the portable tray next to the bed. I pushed the emergency button on the side of my bed and waited for a nurse to come. The nurse was a tall blond woman, about 5ft. with wire rimmed glasses who must have been at least 50 years old. I asked her to help me plug my phone in and power it on. The phone read it was almost 3:00 pm. And then I Unlocked the phone with one hand, typing 1,2,3,4,5 into it. I had angled it on the tray towards me so I could have easier access to it. Once the screen popped on, I felt my heart drop as I looked at a picture of Me, Tristan and Christine on the background of the phone. I felt my eyes water as tears rolled down my cheeks. I almost wanted to throw the phone into a wall but I was still too weak to even rage. All I could think was, why, God why did you take away my family and didn't even give me the privilege to be with them in death. I waited for 20 minutes after crying to use the phone number that Courtney gave me to call her. After the fourth ring she answered the phone.

"Hello?" Courtney asked.

"Hello, is this Courtney?" I asked.

"Yes, this is she." She answered.

"Hi, this is Shane, "I said. "I was wondering if you could take me up on that offer of watching some boxing with me. There's a big fight with a friend of mine that is boxing tonight on ESPN. If it's not too straight forward."

"Well, I would be interested, but I have to watch my daughter tonight," Courtney said. "I don't have a sitter."

"I wouldn't mind meeting your daughter," I said. "I'm pretty lonely here since I am not from Vegas. All of my relatives live in

Duluth, MN right now. My Dad lives in town but I have to pull his arm just to get him here, when it's bingo night."

"If you don't mind, then it's a date Mr. Avis," Courtney said. "I shall be there by 7:30 tonight since that's the normal time for the fights. I did find a bible for you also."

"Thank you so much Courtney," I said. "I look forward to meeting your daughter."

"Get some rest until then Shane," Courtney said then hung up.

Chapter Three

I put the phone down as the tall blond nurse came in with a catheter bag and tube so I knew what was about to happen next. The tube was inserted in my penis and I gasped in pain for a moment. The whole procedure took about five minutes but it sure was painful and uncomfortable, it felt longer than five minutes. After the nurse was done, she turned to me.

"Mr. Avis, your supper will be up shortly," she said.

I nodded. "Thank you for letting me know."

My phone rang and I hurried as fast as I could to unlock it with one hand then hit speaker phone on it.

"Hey kiddo, this is your old man, have you been holding up; ok?" My father said.

"I am as good as I can be until the casts get off and I can use both arms," I said.

"Alright, hang in there, I got your medical insurance information to the doctors and remember we have kept up on the payments since you were in the hospital ok," Don said. "Tomorrow I am going to come visit you so we can go over a plan so you're not in debt before you get healed up alright."

"Yeah, sounds fine to me, since you know about real estate, I would like to get a cheaper place and sell the car," I said. "Since it might take some time to get back into driving."

"Good idea, tomorrow we go over the details and I will try to get it to happen," Don said.

"Thanks Dad, I appreciate it," I said.

"You just get better son and remember we will get you out of there, ok," Don said. "OK, got to let you go since me and your mom will be doing some bingo soon."

"Ok have a good night dad," I said and then he hung up.

I looked at the time on the phone and it read 5:30 PM, my belly was actually starting to growl when the tall blond nurse stepped in with the dinner cart. It was the same type as lunch, mashed potatoes and meat gravy with Jell-O. This time the nurse didn't even hang around and I ate alone with the tv going. After about 30 minutes, she stepped in saw that I was done and asked if I needed anything. I just had her help me move the bed up so I was in a sitting position and able to see the tv better. I kept the channel on ESPN, watching some pro basketball until 7 PM hit then they started with boxing announcers talking about the matchups were about to happen. All of a sudden, I could smell the Lavender perfume and I looked to the door to see Courtney in Jeans, V-Neck grey t-shirt, white tennis shoes, carrying a big purse, her breasts looked like they may leap out of her shirt. She had in tow a 6-year-old girl who was cute, with pigtails, brunette hair, wearing a She-Ra shirt, blue jeans and tennis shoes, carrying a coloring book and crayons. I smiled as they entered the room.

"I'm so glad you could make it Courtney," I said. "I didn't think you would show."

"I don't mind at all being her Shane," she said. "I even remembered the bible that you asked for."

She had pulled an extra chair from a far corner so could to near the bed so the little girl could sit close to us. Courtney pulled out of her big purse a Bible but once I looked closely it looked like a comic book but thick. She handed it to me and I looked it over, it was a comic book bible with all the stories in it.

"Thank you, Courtney, this even better than the normal Bible," I said and placed it on my bed.

"Shane, I would like you to meet Cinderella Ray my beautiful daughter," she said. "I just call her Ella.

Courtney was so close to me with her Angelic smile and beauty, I was hard pressed not to try and kiss her but restrained myself and gave Ella a big smile.

"It's so nice to meet you Ella," I said.

She just smiled shyly and colored in her She-Ra coloring book then a fight was about to start, two lightweight fighters.

"Did work go fast enough for you?" I asked.

"Yes, it was quite uneventful, which I do prefer," Courtney said. "I'm sure you had a long day today."

"I actually had my trainer come by and the boxing physician we use at the fights," I said. "Plus, all of the reading material I got from them should keep me busy for a while."

She pointed at the screen. "Wow, a knockdown already and in the first round."

I looked up to see the black guy get knocked down from the white guy, where the referee started the count down. The black guy got up after the count of 6 then the referee asked the fighter if he was able to go on then the fight started again. Courtney's left hand lay near the mine on the bed. We continued watching the first fight and remarkably the black guy ended up winning in the end with a knockout. Ella interrupted Courtney before she could speak to me and showed her coloring book to her mom.

"That is very good baby," Courtney said. "Maybe someday you can be a painter."

I looked at a picture of She-Ra which actually colored as close as the cartoon and no messes which was extraordinary for a six-year-old girl. I smiled at her.

"That is a really good picture you did Ella." I spoke. "You have a good artistic talent."

Ella smiled. “Thank you, sir.”

She went back to coloring another picture of her book as the next fight was announced, a middleweight matchup between two Hispanics. For some reason while watching the fight my hand found Courtneys, it was a soft hand. She didn’t say anything until one of the fighter’s started bleedings from a cut to the eye.

“Well, if they can’t stop the cut they might shut the match down,” she said.

“Wow, I totally agree with you,” I said. “We will see if the guy takes advantage of the cut to the other opponents eye.”

We watched the two Hispanic men dance around again, one was in red trunks and the other in black. The one in black trunks had the cut formed on his eye, the guy in red was trying to get as many jabs to connect to the wound to open it up again. It was bleeding again profusely, making the guy in the black trunks on the defensive for the whole round. I could feel her hand stroking my fingers. It gave me shivers up my back and I enjoyed the smell of Lavender perfume with being so close to her. The next round the guy in the red trunks opened up the cut bigger and more blood poured out. The referee stopped the fight and had the physician step into the ring to check on the cut. After a few moments looking at it, they stopped the fight pissing the guy off in the black trunks. I looked at Ella.

“Ella, do you like boxing,” I asked.

Ella shook her head. “No, it’s too bloody for me, sir.”

I smiled. “Your right it’s pretty bloody, you can call me Shane.”

“Ok Shane,” Ella said then went back to coloring.

I looked at Courtney and gave her a light squeeze. “The next fight should be on by 9 so Ella won’t be up too late.”

“It’s alright, it usually takes her until 10 to get tired anyways, even on school nights,” Courtney said.

“Are you ok with this?” I asked. “This is pretty abnormal to be watching some boxing with a patient.”

She smiled. “Right now, I am just Courtney, hanging out with my friend Shane and keeping him company.”

I smiled back. “Thank you, Courtney.”

“No problem, Shane,” Courtney said then looked at her watch.” Baby it’s time to take your meds.

Courtney got up. “I’m going to grab some water and plastic cups from the nurse’s station, be right back.”

I nodded as she walked out of the room.” How’s your next picture coming along, Ella?”

Ella stopped then came over to the bed with the coloring book, showing me a colored in picture of Bow on a horse using his bow ironically.

“That’s very good Ella, he was my favorite cartoon character from that show,” I said.

“Thank you, Shane,” Ella said. “I like She-Ra the best since she has a sword.”

“She was one tough chick right,” I chuckled.

Courtney walked in with a plastic jug of water and some cups in her hands, she took the other portable tray from the other side of the room where usually there is another bed. I got lucky for some reason and have been stuck here by myself since I got to the hospital, she rolled it over to us and poured some water in the 3 cups. Courtney took a pill box from her purse and got the pills out for Ella so she could take them. Ella took the pills one at a time, there was just commentary on the last fight as she did that. I felt at that time for some reason God didn’t fail me or was trying to tell me he was going to give something to live for. I know for some reason I was in love with Courtney. She was totally different from the women I used to date, all skinny or like model shape. Christine was a marathon runner so when I wasn’t fighting, I was running with her and going to marathons around the U.S. to see her run. It seemed like I lost one family and found another to keep living. Once Courtney finished helping Ella, she sat back down beside me and grabbed my hand.

"I was wondering, do you have family here in Vegas?" I asked.

"No, it's just me and Ella, I followed my boyfriend Travis to Vegas so he could pursue being a professional card player," Courtney said. "Then he got in drugs and everything went downhill."

"I'm sorry Courtney," I said, squeezing her hand lightly.

I caught glimpse of the next fight and it showed coming up was Darius" Sweet Daddy" Williams going against Tito "El Diablo" Alvarez to be a contender in the light Heavyweight championship of the world. They were in the middle of the ring as the referee was talking to the both fighters about fighting clean. Darius looked pretty muscular and had a big 70's afro with side chops but Tito did not look like some wimp he had the athletic look that was not as pronounced as Darius' build. I pointed out my trainer, Physician and manager to Courtney and Ella.

"Those are my friends that stopped by today and visited," I said. "I am just hoping the manager can do that tomorrow."

Courtney nodded. "This fight looks like it will be evenly matched."

The bell rang and Darius started doing a Muhammad Ali dance around the ring, flicking lightning jabs at Tito's face. He connected once in a while to the body and then the jabs to the head for the first round, trying to feel him out. I took a drink from my cup of water then settled my hand back into Courtney's. The second round went the same way but Tito began finally started getting a few punches into Darius, making the match more exciting now. By the fifth round I could see Tito was starting to tire, his punches lacked power. Darius had given a cut to Tito's right eye and then a big uppercut that knocked him down. Courtney got up and yelled for a second. It was exciting to see a woman who actually liked boxing since Christine barely liked watching them, the first time was basically the end.

"I'm sorry, I usually watch boxing and wrestling," Courtney said. "And sometimes I really get into it, isn't that right Ella."

"Yes, mommy sometimes throws stuff at the tv if her fighter doesn't win," Ella said.

I laughed. "Wow, such violence Courtney and enthusiasm, I like it. I hope when I get back into the ring you will be there cheering me on."

She smiled and squeezed my hand. "I hope I will be there too Shane."

Chapter four

Courtney

When I first strolled in with the cart and I saw Shane I thought to myself what a handsome man, even with a few tubes coming out of his body. I could tell from his eyes he really was turned on by me for some reason. I'm a big girl, at least 180 pounds even though I work hard and rarely eat really heavy. I am pretty sure the late-night ice cream and some chocolate never helped but my buttocks and hips are wide. Glasses of course, without them I would be blind as a bat but I took care of my make-up and hair as best I could. I had been praying to God after Travis died from the overdose Meth that I would find someone that would love me for who I was. A man that would not care if I didn't look like a super model. I had found out about a month ago Shane was in the ICU in a coma after his car accident. A semi-truck rammed him and his family off the road on a rainy night after his big win. I would go in and have to relieve his bladder and I would see his penis erect from my touch and it was over the average the male size. It was bigger than Travis' had but of course after inserting the tube it would shrink from the pain of the tube going in. When I had to just clean up behind a nurse, I could see it did not get erect when touched. When Shane looked at me it was intense like I was the only focus in the room. I had almost freaked, when I got a call from Shane at my home. I knew as a professional he should not be alone but also, I just wanted to be around him. Ella didn't mind coming with, as long as she could do her coloring which she really enjoyed. I had showered and shaved my legs then put some of my lavender perfume on in between my breasts. I put the casual clothes on so I would not feel like it was a real date but it sure felt like it. Shane touched my hand, it sent shivers up my spine and made me wet between my legs almost. He couldn't stop holding my hand and that made me feel like a million bucks for some reason. I just hoped this would continue, for me and him, it would be a long recovery for Shane but I could see he had desire to get better and be whole again. After Tito was knocked down, it took him the count of five before getting up. The bell rang and they were able to go to their corners. Before the bell sounded, the doctor came out and looked at Tito's eye which he nodded his head to the ref, he was in shape enough to still fight. The bell rang for round six and both men when at each other like madmen.

"This is it; I think if Darius can put some more power punches into the fight, he maybe be able to knock him down again," Shane said.

"Your probably right, since the Hispanic guy is running out of gas," I said.

Darius kept circling and getting in his jab then out of nowhere he popped two uppercuts under Tito's chin that put him to the mat. The ref jumped in and started the countdown and then for some reason began counting too. Shane looked at me and grinned, started counting with me. Tito could not get up and the ref called ten and the crowd went wild, then the tall blond nurse, Lisa walked into the room with a frown.

"Can you please keep it down, you're disturbing the other patients Courtney," she said.

"Oh, sorry Lisa, I didn't mean to upset anybody," I said. "The fight is over with now anyways."

"Ok, good and Shane do you need anything yet?" Lisa asked

Shane shook his head no." I'm good but thanks for asking. What time do I have to do the catheter deal?'

"In an hour," she said. "Or you can do it right after Courtney leaves."

Shane looked to me and said." Courtney, could you have Ella step out of the room for a few minutes to get it done. I would prefer you to be with me."

I looked at him surprised but said. "That's fine Shane, I can stay for you, Ella could you step over by the bathroom, we are going to use the curtain."

Ella nodded and got out of the big recliner, walking over to the bathroom while I pulled the curtain around Shane. I went with the nurse and got the catheter kit.

"I can do it so you don't have to Lisa, I got it," I said.

"Sure, that's fine but be careful ok," Lisa said. "Just hit the emergency button if you need me."

I walked back into the room, just stopping by Ella for a moment." I will be quick as possible Ella, Ok."

Ella nodded." Ok, momma"

I went behind the curtain and set the kit on the bed then got it ready to be used, putting a glob of Vaseline on the tube. I grabbed Shane's penis and like before it sparked an erection from my touch.

"OK, get ready, maybe close your eyes and take a deep breath," I said.

I inserted the tube in to the Urethra hole and heard a sharp exhale from Shane as his penis shrunk from the pain a bit. I started getting urine into the bag until it was totally filled then I pulled out the tube and cleaned the area. I pulled Shane's medical gown down then put the urine waste in the bathroom. I smiled at my daughter.

"It's all done, Ella, you can go sit back in the chair ok," I said.

I pulled the curtain back for Shane so he could see the tv again and of course me, also Ella. He smiled weakly at me, for some reason I wanted to kiss him then but I restrained myself.

"Thank you, now I can wait until morning," he said.

I smiled and patted his good arm." Not a problem, Shane. I probably should get Ella home so she can get some sleep for school."

"Alright, I just want to thank you again for your company, Courtney and you Ella," Shane smiled, pointing at Ella.

Ella giggled. "I have a picture for you Shane."

Ella walked over to Shane and handed him a colored phot of Bow from She-Ra cartoon that she had worked on. Shane's eyes had some tears roll down his face as she gave him a quick hug.

"Thank you, Ella," Shane said.

I couldn't help myself but I kissed Shane on the forehead instead of giving in temptation and kissing him on the lips. He was a little surprised but it brought a smile to his face.

"Will I see you at Lunch again?" Shane asked.

I smiled. "Yes, I will be serving you again at lunch. We can talk more tomorrow."

"Alright, have a good night, Courtney," Shane said.

I waved and so did Ella as we walked out of the room and into the maze of hallways to get to the elevator. Once we got in the elevator, I pressed the button to get to the ground floor then I looked at Ella.

"So, what did you think of Shane?" I asked.

"He's a nice guy momma," Ella said.

"Yes, he is," I said.

The elevator opened up on the bottom floor and I took Ella's hand and guided her the rest of the way out to the parking lot. We headed to our Dodge Mini-van that I had that was from 2005 and I unlocked my driver side door so I could hit unlock on all doors. I went around and opened the passenger side door for the back so I could put Ella in her booster seat. I closed the door so it would shut then got into the driver seat.

"Momma, will we see Shane ever again?" Ella asked

"I think we will honey, "I said.

"Good, because he seems nice," Ella said.

I smiled in the darkness of the vehicle as we drove away from the hospital and towards our trailer home on the outskirts of town. Once I got into the maze of the streets in the trailer community, I parked in front of the place I was renting. It wasn't the worse for renting, like about 900 a month and trash with utilities. The outside needed a paint job but the inside I made sure was clean and kept up. I unlocked the door as Ella followed behind me to get inside the place. I shut and locked the door behind me with two locks as Ella headed straight to her bedroom.

"Ella, don't forget to brush your teeth before bed, honey," I said.

"Ok Momma," she called back.

I went to my bedroom and went inside, it wasn't that big since I gave Ella the bigger bedroom, I had just a single bed, a dresser, closet and a bookshelf. I did have a small computer desk with a laptop on it and a 25-inch tv with tv stand decorating the room. I pulled off all my clothes except my socks then pulled on a night shirt that had sponge-bob on the front. I went into Ella's room to go tuck her in and give her a kiss goodnight. Ella was laying in her small racing bed that was Lightning McQueen from Disney. I leaned over to kiss her cheek then pulled the covers over her.

"Goodnight Cinderella, sweet dreams," I said.

Ella closed her eyes and I left the room, closing the door behind me as I went back to my bedroom. I closed my door behind me and shut the light off, grabbing my cellphone from a nightstand next to the bed. I began searching on the media platforms and found Shane on Facebook, sending him a friend request from my profile. Then I searched for images of him on the google app and came up with a whole bunch of fight pictures of Shane. He looked so ripped and handsome in them it made my heart flutter. I saved at least three on my phone and put one on my screensaver background and one of Ella. I set it down and stared at the ceiling for a while then I began my prayer to God.

"Lord, just let this be the one person I have been searching for and please keep your healing hand on Shane to be whole again," I said. "That's all I ask."

I closed my eyes and hoped I would not have nightmares of Travis, who beat me when he was on drugs. I let myself fall into a peaceful sleep.

Chapter Five

Shane

I felt like I was in high school all over again, I had a nice giddy feeling when I was always around Courtney with her beautiful angelic face. I felt kind of depressed that she had to leave but it was really late for Ella and visiting hours were over. I know it was kind of wrong because they say you should grieve from losing your loved ones but she seemed to be my rock. I would try to take everything slow and focus on healing so I could train again. It was probably close to eleven O'clock when my cellphone buzzed and, on a Facebook, request was from Courtney. I unlocked my phone and opened the request using the free WI-FI from the hospital. It was a nice picture of Courtney with a beautiful smile and wearing plastic pink framed glasses on, with her huge bosom showing through her V-neck t-shirt. After I accepted her friend request, I looked through her photos and found a picture of her Ella at a fair, standing near a Ferris wheel. I saved the photo on my phone then put it on my home screen, the other was of Tristan and Christine, my only photo on the phone of them. I couldn't understand why God would take away one family then give me another. I knew Courtney was attracted to me as much as I was of her but maybe for me more since I loved her face. I made sure no one was walking by, when I put in a prayer with God, asking for healing and what I should do with Courtney. After that I began just channel surfing, when Lisa the tall blond nurse stopped in the room.

"Can I get you anything Mr. Avis?" she asked.

"Do you know if Courtney is seeing anyone seriously? "I asked. "I know you might not be able to answer but I thought I would ask."

"I was really surprised to see her here tonight, she normally doesn't even talk to patients," she said. "I know one guy tried asking her out here and she flat out said no."

"Ok, thank you, that's all I wanted to know." I spoke.

She smiled." Your, welcome."

She left the room and for some reason I felt flush and happy from hearing what she said about Courtney. It was about another hour then I felt tired enough to shut off the tv and fall into a peaceful sleep. The night went by really fast and all of a sudden, I was woken up by a nurse to empty my bladder. Then a therapist came in we began on working on self- care, using a body wipe then brushing teeth. They even let me use an electric shaver to clean up my face since I had a ratty beard going. We also went over some writing skills and reading to see if I remembered much from the coma. They also setup another time they would be coming to do the same stuff with me so I would get into a routine. By the time the therapist got done it was almost lunch time. The lady left then Courtney came in wearing her scrubs and pushing a lunch cart with the same food from the other day. I smiled at her as she set the tray on the portable tray holder.

"You look a lot younger since you got all cleaned up," Courtney said with a smile.

"I feel a lot better now since I have been trying to keep up my grooming again," I said. "Did Ella get to bed alright?"

"Yes, she fell fast asleep, once she got home," Courtney said.

"I accepted your friend request before I went to bed last night," I said. "I was wondering if you still have those pink framed glasses, they really look good on you."

She blushed. "I don't think so but thank you. I had to change prescriptions this year."

I liked when she blushed and her smiled it made my body feel hot and she was close to me as I was eating lunch. I could smell the lavender perfume on her as she sat close.

"I'm glad the therapists have been now starting to work with me so I can at least get myself ready for the recovery center," I said.

"Next Tuesday, you will get all of your casts off, that should be exciting," Courtney said. "You probably will be very sore in your left arm and leg. The neck hopefully won't be too tender, when the brace comes off."

"I expect the pain since I have had some fights where the recovery wasn't fun either," I said.

I had finished my plate and put it on the cart with my good arm, she instantly grabbed a wipe, began cleaning my hands and face. I had the urge to just grab the back of her head and pull her in for a kiss but I stopped myself.

"I was wondering, if on Saturday you and Ella could stop by and play some UNO?" I asked. "I'm sure by then I will get a deck from my old man."

"I will have to think about it since I do work 4 hours during the day," Courtney said. "But I will let you know Saturday after I am done with work."

"That's fine," I said. "I forgot you worked on Saturday also, up to you anyways."

She was about to respond when Darius walked into the room, looked a little weary but not beaten up in anyway. He cracked a big smile on his face.

"Dude! it's it's good to see yaw' bro', it's a miracle after seeing that car after they pulled it from the hill," Darius said.

He was followed by DeMarcus and Evan, they all set more boxing and wrestling magazines on the portable tray that was opposite. Courtney took the dishes from the closest one to me.

“See you, Shane,” Courtney said.

She slipped past the other men with the cart and went out the door. DeMarcus sat down next to me.

“I am really relieved you didn’t end up dead, Shane,” DeMarcus, “You should have waited to travel and came to the after party.”

DeMarcus was in a fancy pink suit and looked like a pimp, he was 6 feet, Black with a handsome suave look to him.

I nodded. “I regret I didn’t man, every day. My family would still be alive if I have,”

All the guys hung there head a little after I said that, a brief silence swept the room until I broke it.

“I get my casts taken off in 3 days,” I said. “Then I will be working on therapy way more than I am now.”

“That’s good to know, the faster you get your body moving the better chance you can start training again,” Evan piped in.

Evan gave me a half- hearted hug. “Listen I got to go pack while you talk to these guys. I really hope you get back to the way you were before.”

I waved to him as he walked out and turned back to DeMarcus. “Listen, I know this is a stretch but, in a year, I should be fully healed. Is there a chance I could get another fight?”

DeMarcus nodded. “I could swing something to the public man. It would be a big comeback just like Vinny Pazienza but at least you don’t have to worry about losing a belt.”

I smiled. “Good, I plan on getting in the best shape of my life and getting a belt.”

“I believe in you homie,” Darius said. “You were a contender for the Middleweight title. There is nothing you can’t do without the help of God; I'll pray for you."

"Thanks Darius and last night was a great fight," I said. "I at least got to watch it on ESPN while being here, I guess."

DeMarcus took out his business card and set it on the portable tray holder.

"I changed my number since I got a different phone service, ok," he said. "Give me a call when you start training again."

He looked at his watch. "Darius, it's time to go finish packing to get ready for the flight. You take it easy Shane; I hope you get better."

Both men stepped out of the room and left me to be alone and I switched on the tv to look for something to watch. I was at least pleased that Darius stopped by since we had hung out a lot and sparred all the time so I could be ready for my fights. It didn't take long before my father showed up with my mother in tow. She gave me a hard hug and the old man put his hand on my shoulder then sat down next to the bed.

"I'm glad you're here Dad, I have a big favor to ask of you," I said.

"What's that kiddo?" Don asked.

"I need you to hire someone to clean out the house of Tristan's and Christine's stuff," I said. "If the parents want anything give it to them. Plus, I need the mansion sold and the Porsche."

His eyes widened. "Are you sure Shane? You're not hurting for money; you have about 500,000 saved in the bank."

I nodded blinking away tears. "Yes, I am sure. And I need you find me like a pre-fab home with a ramp, in case I still have trouble walking once I get out of the hospital."

"All in Duluth though? Maybe here in Vegas?" Don asked.

"We would love to have you stay with us until you get back on your feet," My mother piped up.

"I know you guys would but I want Vinny to train me a little while longer," I said. "I think he will be able to get me some more fights than I can investigate gyms around in Vegas to see if I can get a start in this town."

"Alright, I can do that, I know you use US bank so when I get checks for the extra money from the house and car I can deposit it," My father said.

I opened my phone then checked inside for notes saved like my banking password and gave him the password. I looked at my father.

"I never got my wallet back so If you have it my bank card is still sitting in there," I said.

"Don't worry I will look for it and find the rest of the information," he said. "Just try to get healed up."

"Thanks Dad," I said. "What are you guys up to after visiting me?"

"Probably after making sure, I have your wallet, we plan going to dinner and do some bowling," Dad said.

I nodded, looking at the clock, it read; 2:00 pm. "Well that sounds good, I have my tutoring classes shortly since the coma there working on my memory."

After I said that a therapist walked in, a brunette that was pretty and in shape but not as pretty as Courtney, I definitely had feelings for her.

"Mr. Avis, I have come to do a little studying today," she said.

My mother and father got up, giving me a hug. "We will stop by in a week and I will update you if I get rid of the house and car."

I nodded. "Thanks Dad, I appreciate it."

They both waved then the therapist sat down with a few workbooks and pencils on the portable tray holder.

"Let's get busy Mr. Avis," she said.

I knew it was going to be a long rest of the day.

Chapter six

Courtney

The next two weeks seemed to go by pretty quickly, once Shane got his casts off and extra tube out of his body. He looked even more handsome once he had cleaned up and started taking care of himself better. We seemed to be getting closer to each other as days went by, having at least one Saturday a week of games with Ella and me. We would play UNO or Candyland or Shane would want to do coloring with Ella in her She-Ra book. Shane's range of motion in both arms were getting better with Therapy and even was now using a walker to walk around. I would walk down the hallway and back after he ate lunch. It was about 3 weeks after getting the casts off that they gave him a date of going into a recovery center to get him to do more therapy. Shane looked way healthier and was eating good meals, plus doing some bodyweight exercises that was giving him muscle tone back into his arms. I was just rolling in the cart when I saw Shane's father walk out of the room.

"Oh, sorry, Mr. Avis, I almost ran you over there," I said. "How is Shane doing today?"

"Oh, very good! I just got him about 550,000 dollars put in the bank for him," Don said. "I sold his mansion and Porsche the other day so he could get a different house."

"Oh, Wow," I said. "He is lucky to have you as a father. I better get him his lunch, have a nice day."

He smiled. "You too Courtney."

He headed off down the hall and I completed rolling the cart into the room and Shane looked over with a great smile on his face.

“There's that Gorgeous nurse I have been missing so much,” he said. “How you doing today?”

I blushed as he said that.” I am doing very well Shane; I see your father gave you some good news?”

He nodded. “I did get some good news and as I eat, I have a business proposition for you if you will hear me out.”

I sat down and took off the tray cover of his lunch what consisted of Meatloaf, mashed potatoes and mixed vegetables. He took it and set it in front of him with the portable tray, looking at me hopefully. I raised an eyebrow.

“OK, what is this business proposition Shane?” I asked.

“It would be life altering for you and Ella but you would make 1,200 every 2 weeks tax free money, a roof over your head and free food,” Shane said. “I am asking for help from you, it would be around the house until I got myself up and running. Which I plan on doing since I want to box again and get me to my doctor's appointments until I can drive again.”

My head was in a spin, it was almost like Shane asked me to marry him, it definitely was life altering like Shane said. Granted, I had no family here to tie me down and I wasn't married or even a boyfriend but this would take some thought.

“I would have to talk to Ella and think about it Shane,” I said. “That is life altering.”

Shane nodded. “I understand Courtney and hope you will consider it as a friend. The new place I have is a 3 bedroom and a ramp in case I am still using a walker. It's a decent home and it will be in a better part of Duluth since it's next to the Miller Hill Mall.”

“I only make 1600 every 2 weeks so it wouldn't be the worse especially if I had a place, I wasn't making the rent payments with my own checkbook," I said.

"You do not have to make a decision yet, I will have 5 more weeks of therapy at the recovery center in Vegas," Shane said. "Then I will have to get a ride or flight back to Duluth anyways to get settled into the new place."

"I will talk to Ella tonight and hopefully give you an answer before you leave from this hospital," I said. "I have no family here in Vegas, most of my relatives and parents live in Northern Iowa."

Shane finished eating his food and closed up the tray then asked me to get him upright so he could use the walker to follow me down the hall. I did that then he took his phone out and I caught a glimpse of a photo of me and Ella standing in front of a Ferris wheel smiling for the camera. It gave my heart a kick to see he really liked me and Ella to having a picture of us on his phone. I mean for a normal person it should have been creepy but for me, Shane seemed really sincere in having in interest in me and my family. He wrote his number down a scrap piece of paper and handed it to me before we started our walk.

"This is just in case you miss me before the deadline," he said. "I really will need the help in the months I get out of the recovery center."

I took the scrap of paper from Shane and set it in my front pocket of my scrub pants then began rolling the cart out into the hallway. Shane followed as best he could with his generic walker that the hospital uses to stay close to me.

"How is Ella doing in school?" Shane asked.

"She's doing really well in first grade, getting along with the other kids and doing well in all the reading, writing, and math they have in that grade," I said.

"That's great, I know Tristan had a hard time while going to school with his autism that he had," Shane said. "I had a special tutor for him to get through the first and second grade."

I could see his face drop from being in a great mood to a sad mood after he finished saying that, like his heart was breaking. I wanted to give him a hug but I needed to get the other lunches out to a few more patients. I pushed the button for the floor I needed at the elevator.

"I will try to call you this Saturday on your phone," I said.

"That sounds great, thanks again Courtney," Shane said. "Have a good rest of your day."

I gave him a quick hug then pushed the cart into the elevator to get away from Shane so he wouldn't see the tears roll down my face. The elevator doors closed and I hurried up and wiped my eyes with a napkin from Shane's tray. I knew he still was crushed by losing his family and I hoped he wasn't just trying to use me and Ella as a substitute. I was hoping his offer was genuine so we could get out of the trailer home and into a real home. The weather would be just as unpredictable as Iowa weather that I grew up with but I bet Ella would like the snow. Shane seemed genuine and really interested in me and Ella, when most guys blew me off once they had heard I had a kid. Most of the time they just wanted a one-night stand so I would just disappear on the date and go home. I kept thinking about the pros and Cons of moving out of Vegas and there were pros than cons. I finished with all of the lunches and then I was cleaning the carts off, I bumped into Lisa as I was finishing up and she was just getting ready for her shift.

"Hi, Lisa, how you been?" I asked.

She looked at me with a smile. "How about you? I heard you caught that hunk of a boxer's eye. He can't stop asking about you. He blows off all the single nurses that hit on him."

I flushed slightly. "I just have been being nice to him on Saturday's since he only has his folks living here and they barely visit."

"Well, if you ask me, he would be the guy you would want to marry," Lisa said. "He's almost a millionaire. He has such a fighting spirit; he is finally starting to heal fast."

"I noticed," I said. "Lisa, he has asked me to work for him in Minnesota for almost the same amount I make here with free room and board. What do you think I should do?"

Lisa gave me a big smile. "See, that guy can't get enough of you. Courtney. You have a young girl that needs a better life than being around in the city of sin if you ask me. I think maybe you should give love a chance. God is pointing you towards this for some reason."

"I will pray about it when I get home," I said.

"You do that, I will let Shane know you said hi to make his day," Lisa said.

I smiled. "You're crazy, but you do that as long as it makes him happy."

Lisa left me alone and I went to the locker room to change into street clothes so I could pick up Ella from her elementary school. I shut the locker door then went out to the hospital parking lot, where my silver 2010 Dodge mini-van was parked. I got in and started it up then headed to Ella's elementary school was at. By the time I got there, I was waiting in line as the doors to the school let out with screaming kids running out. Ella found my van right away; she was wearing jeans and a She-Ra t-shirt with tennis shoes. She liked the new She-Ra show so much she had at least 2 shirts hanging up. I hit the automatic side door so she could get into her booster seat in the back of the van. This van had a DVD player hanging in the back so she could watch a few different shows or movies I had on DVD. Ella buckled in as I turned on the DVD player from the front, near the dashboard.

"So baby, how was your day? "I asked as we drove away from school.

"It was fun, we actually had a craft day," Ella said. "We made a picture of how we wanted our family to be."

"That's nice dear, when you get home you can show me," I said.

It took forty minutes from the school to the trailer park we lived in, going by the highway so Ella watched two shows of Sponge bob in the back. I turned into our little parking space next to the mobile home, parking the vehicle. I opened the side door then I got out and close my door locking it as Ella unbuckled from the booster seat. I helped Ella down and could hear the people from the mobile home across from us yelling at each other. I closed the side door and peeked over at the mobile and saw a man and woman yelling, the woman threw a beer can at him.

"Come on Ella, let's get inside quick," I said.

I pulled her up the small stairs to the front door and unlocked it, getting her into the house then locked the door behind me. I set my purse on the kitchen table since it was right next to the living room.

"Ella, go change into your pajamas and I am going to make dinner," I said.

Ella went down the small hallway, all the way back where her room was to go change into her other clothes. I went into the kitchen and opened one of the cupboards, pulling out Kraft macaroni and cheese. I got medium saucepan out, putting water into the pan then set it on the stove. Ella came into the kitchen carrying a drawing of some sort on a piece of paper and set it on the kitchen table while the water boiled. I put the macaroni into boiling water then stopped to look at the picture. It was an actual decent drawing of a house with a man, woman and child stood in front.
"So, what's this Ella?" I asked.

"That's Shane, you and me mommy," Ella said.

My heart fluttered as she said that and scared me a little as I responded. "That's nice baby."

I went to the fridge and pulled out hot dogs from the freezer then stuck them into another saucepan with water in it. I set it on the stove and turned the electric burner on high so the water could begin to cook. I turned around and looked at Ella.

"I have an important question for you Ella," I said. "Shane has asked me to help him recover from his injuries. Basically, we would have to move in summer to Minnesota but it would be closer to Grandma and Grandpa in Iowa. What do you think about that?"

Ella's face lightened up. "You mean we would be living with Shane. That would be awesome, I would miss my friends but I would really like that!"

"We would be living with Shane so you could see him every day," I said. "If I say yes, you won't be mad?"

Ella smiled. "No momma, I won't be mad I'll be happy. I think you will be happy too."

I smiled back. "You might be right dear. Let me finish dinner then we can go watch one of your shows."

I finished dinner then set up our plates with a few hot dogs then put macaroni and cheese on our plates. We ate in silence but Ella made funny faces at me so I would laugh. I knew she had a real connection with Shane when he would make her his center of attention, for some reason I would get all hot and bothered by it. We finished dinner then I did the dishes right away as Ella picked one of her movies out. I sat down next to her on our black Futon couch and we sat watching on our 25-inch flat screen, The Incredibles. I felt pretty good that we would be getting out of this crappy trailer park and I would be with both the people I wanted to be with. I picked up my Samsung cellphone and I sent a text message.

Courtney: Shane we will move with you to Minnesota. Please don't make me regret this.

I set the phone down on the coffee table as Ella and I finished watching the Incredibles both of us laughing at some of the antics happening on screen. When we finished, it was eight PM so I let Ella pick a She-Ra show to watch until nine. I then put Ella in bed and I put my pajamas on so I could relax before bed. I looked at the sexy photo of Shane with his muscles rippling in his boxing trunks from a promotion poster I found. I set the phone down and prayed.

"God, please let me know if my decision is wrong or if it's right before the move," I whispered.

I then let myself fall into blissful sleep and dreamed of Shane.

Chapter Seven

Shane

While I was watching the Big Bang Theory, I saw my phone go off and the lock screen of Courtney showed up with a text message. I opened the phone to see Courtney's message. I typed a text message in return.

Shane: You won't regret this Courtney, thank you.

I sent the message in return and felt a smile on my face, I was like a little kid in a candy store or just maybe falling in love. I felt weird since I know should keep showing grief for my other family but would they want me to be alone that was the question. I think Christine would have wanted me to move on at some point. It already had been 4 months and will be over 5 months by the time I get to live back in Duluth. I actually felt the urge to urinate and now begin doing that on my own but I had to turn the faucet on to help. I pushed the emergency button and Lisa stopped into the room.

"I need help to get into the restroom," I said.

"Ok Mr. Avis," she said.

She came around where the walker was and helped me stand then I used the walker to get to the bathroom. I turned the faucet on then positioned myself over the toilet so I could stay standing without falling. I only closed the door part way in case of an emergency was about to happen then I relaxed, the urine spraying freely. After I got done, I fixed my medical gown then washed my hands before heading back to the bed. Lisa helped me get set properly on the bed and then put the walker to the side.

"I bet it feels good to at least go to the bathroom on your own," Lisa said.

"It sure does, I don't enjoy something rammed up my penis on a daily basis," I said. "I want to be able to use it at some point."

"I understand Mr. Avis," she chuckled. "If you don't need anything else, have a good night."

While watching ESPN again I was doing triceps exercise on the bed, lifting my skinny frame and doing about ten reps a piece. A different nurse stepped in the room past midnight to check on me.

"I'm not jerking off, just doing some strengthening pushups on the bed," I said watching tv.

"Don't worry I wasn't thinking that," she said.

I looked over at her, she was about 5'7ft. tall with model's body and face with red hair but she still did not turn me on like Courtney did.

"Just came to see if you needed anything before, I started my paperwork," she said.

"I'm good, I am just about to go to bed honestly," I said and shut the tv off.

She nodded her head and shut one of the lights off. "Goodnight, Mr. Avis."

There was less light in the room and I tried to relax and let myself fall asleep but then I started having the nightmare. I was driving in the pouring rain on the windy roads near Lake Mead and the truck smashing into the rental car. It put us into a spin as we screamed and smashed into the railing then toppled over as I flew out of the car. I must have screamed as I woke up, the nurse came running into the room.

"Mr. Avis!" she yelled.

I couldn't breathe and it scared me. "I can't breathe.'

Tears rolled down my cheeks as I tried to settle down from the nightmare, the nurse tried to lower me forward and rub my back. She had an oxygen tank next to the bed and she put the mask on my face.

"Mr. Avis, try to take slow breaths," she said. "You must have had a nightmare sir, just take it easy."

I breathed slowly and took deep breaths to get myself back to normal and my heart went back to normal in a few minutes. The fresh oxygen helped me get calm, I must have had a panic attack after the nightmare. The nurse sat with me for a few more minutes than I just turned on the tv again.

"I'll stay up longer, hopefully I will fall asleep again," I said.

"If you need anything just hit the button and I will come in to help," she said.

I nodded. "Thank you."

I watched tv for a while then must have dozed off with no nightmares or dreams for the rest of the night. It was about nine AM that I was awaken by the nurse with my breakfast, it was some eggs, bacon and toast. I ate it eagerly then the therapist came into work with me on standing up from the bed, we did this ten times. We did range of motion stuff with my arms to counteract the stiffness. They were getting better and less sore from all the stretching that was being done. I knew I only had one more day at the hospital which kind of depressed me since I wouldn't see Courtney or Ella as often as I had. We got done with range of motion then went over basic math and writing, reading skills. Before lunch I had one of the nurses help me get a shower in then I used the electric shave to stay clean. I was just getting done when Courtney walked in with the lunch cart. A smile formed on my face.

"Hey Courtney, I'm glad you said yes," I said moving the tray holder closer to me.

She smiled. “You can thank Ella when you see her Saturday for boardgame night. She is one happy little girl.”

“I will indeed do that,” I said as she set the tray in front of me. “How was your day yesterday?”

“Well, the neighbors scared the hell out of us, with their fighting, “Courtney said. “I think one of the other people called the cops to get rid of them. But once I asked her about moving, she was super excited, the rest of the night was a piece of cake.”

“That’s great, I was doing alright until I went to sleep then I had a nightmare about the accident,” I said. “I scared the night nurse who was on duty.”

She touched my arm then grabbed my hand which gave me shivers up my spine, the smell of Lavender comforted me.

“I’m sorry Shane,” Courtney said. “So, after Sunday, they will transport you to the recovery center, right?”

“Yes, and get me settled in then I will do more therapy work on doing common household tasks,” I said. “I am still trying to get my left foot to work better, it still has drop foot.”

“They have weights at the recovery center, maybe that will help,” Courtney said.

“I hope so,” I said as I finished my lunch. “I want a few more fights before I begin training anyone for boxing.”

“That’s what you want to do?” Courtney asked.

“Yeah, have a gym and train some but maybe get a full entourage exercise studios going,” I said.

“Sounds like a good idea,” she said as she put the tray on the lunch cart.

Courtney helped me stand up so I could use the walker so I could shuffle down the hall with her to the elevators.

“So, what game would you like to play on Saturday? Bring chutes and ladders or Candyland?" I asked.

"I can bring both if you want," she said.

We came to a stop by the elevator and Courtney picked the floor she needed to go to as I gave her a hug. It sent an electric shock through my body as we touched, an almost instant arousal for me. I quickly stepped back.

"I hope you have a good rest of your day Courtney," I said.

She blushed "You too Shane."

The elevators opened and she went inside, I did a quick wave before the doors closed to the elevator. I shuffled back down the hall to my room and then positioned myself to get back into bed using my arms. I was just getting ready to switch the tv on, when my father walked into the room with a smile on his face.

"Hey, Champ, how you doing? My father asked. "I saw you were up and rolling with the walker."

"Yeah, I am at least now getting up and down with a little less help from the Nurses," I said.

"That's great and I also have some more great news," Don said. "The trucking company has given you a settlement of 500,00 dollars since they don't want to go to court since they know the truck driver was in the wrong."

My eyes widened." Wow, that's great to hear pops. I'm glad you're helping me out."

"No problem kiddo. I'm just glad your alive ok. Everything else have been going good for you?" he said.

"Well, I hired a nurse for when I am in Duluth," I said. "Once I get a few big fights then I will be looking into getting a fitness center open in Vegas."

My father sat next to the bed. "So why don't you do that now? Get yourself back into shape and run a gym."

"Because I was so close to being champion and that's what Vinny can do for me, he can get me the middleweight championship," I said. "It's been my dream as a kid dad."

"I get it but don't be disappointed if you don't make it," Don said. "Your body right now is pretty screwed up; it will definitely take you a year to heal."

"I get what your saying, keep my expectations low so if failure occurs, it's not so bad," I said.

"Yes, and keep your idea about the gym so if you don't get a championship fight, you have that for back up," my father said.

"I will dad, not a problem there," I said.

Don stood up. "What nurse is going to be staying with you? Three bedrooms enough for the house?"

I smiled. "Courtney will be moving with me to Duluth and probably drive me there."

He nodded. "Just remind her that there will be already furniture there and beds."

"If you can have Tristan's race car, put in one of the bedrooms that would be good, Courtney has a daughter," I said.

"Got it kiddo, you just keep trying to heal up," My father said.

Don left the room and I was left all alone again with the TV so I started channel surfing for a bit then stopped back on ESPN. I kept thinking myself at least I am worth a million bucks, I would have to make sure the insurance company had paid out so I could bury the wife and kid. Then I remembered it had since I had been stuck in the hospital when the funeral went for both of them. It hurt like hell, I was almost an invalid and couldn't even attend my wife's and son's funeral. I touched the emergency button on the side of the medical bed and Lisa the blonde nurse showed up.

"Can I help you, Shane?" she asked.

"Can you help me to the bathroom?" I asked.

She helped me stand up then I used the walker that was next to the bed to walk to the bathroom. I relieved myself then washed my hands in the sink, I walked out of the bathroom, stopping to ask something of Lisa.

"I want to walk to the nurse's station and back if you don't mind," I said. "Just to keep me moving."

"Sure, that's fine," she said.

I walked near her as we headed to the station that wasn't too far away and I was thinking about the coming weeks. I needed to push my body harder to get my strength back so I could take care of myself and Courtney. Once we got to the station, I turned myself around and we headed back to my room. I was tired by the time we got near the bed and I set it so she could help me get in bed. I pulled myself in with the strength in my arms and set upright so I could watch tv again.

"Thanks Lisa," I said.

"Your welcome Shane, I heard tomorrow they will be transferring you over to the recovery center," Lisa said.

"That is true, at least I will be working harder to walk and stand again," I said. "That's my main goal when I get there."

"That is a good first goal, when you accomplish that then you can work on training to fight again," Lisa said.

"You got that right," I said.

"Alright, if you need anything just hit the button," Lisa said.

I smiled then switched on the tv. "Thank you."

The rest of the night was fairly calm when I fell into sleep and began dreaming about Courtney.

Chapter Eight

Courtney

The next few weeks went pretty fast for me and Shane as I was packing just the most precious stuff I needed. The rest went to a Savers store or to neighbors who needed furniture for their mobile homes. I would visit Shane on a Saturday and we would have lunch in the rec room with him and when the other patients left for their rooms' we would play a boardgame. He was getting more filled out, from using the weights in the weight room and looked healthier. I knew I was falling in love with Shane and he with me. He treated more like a lover would, hold my hand while playing a game or just watching a tv. It was only a matter of time we would kiss. I didn't know how to feel about that. He would be talking about going someplace for the summer with Ella that would be fun. He was like Travis until he became a drug addict then he changed into a monster but I had a feeling Shane would always be a nice guy. He would always greet us with hugs at the entrance and be interested in everyday activities we had to do for the week. I had put my 2 weeks into the hospital and stopped by with Ella, the week before the move on a Saturday again. Shane was standing at the entrance like always with a big smile on his face.

"My favorite two ladies in the world," Shane said. "How are you guys today?"

"Tired but good," Courtney said.

He startled me when he came and hugged me then went to Ella, giving her a big hug.

"How's my little girl?" Shane said.

"Good papa, I made you another picture," Ella said.

His face was startled and a single tear rolled down his cheek. "I can't wait to see it."

We walked close to each other and headed to the rec room and Ella bounded for it.

"You ok she said that Shane," I said.

He took one hand off his walker and rubbed my back. "Yes Courtney, it's totally fine."

We sat down in our usual spots and ordered what food we wanted with Shane using his credit card or debit card to pay for both of our meals. Shane sat closest to me.

"You've been able to get rid of your furniture and kitchen stuff? I'm sure I have all that at the new house and I got a bed for Ella," Shane said.

"Oh ok, thank you Shane," I said. "We definitely just have to bring our clothes then."

"Should we play some Candyland after lunch, Ella," Shane asked.

"Sure papa, that would be great," Ella said.

The food came and some kitchen workers put all the lunches out by the patients with some nurses helping some of the patients who couldn't use their own forks. We ate in silence for a while, Shane just looking at me and smiling as he was eating. When we finished, the kitchen workers took away the plates and we moved to the table closest to the boardgames. I helped set up the Candyland board, when Ella took out a colored picture of He-Man and She-Ra together, Shane smiled at Ella.

"Thank you, Ella," Shane said.

We started playing the game and having fun, with Ella actually winning two games, there was no stopping her. When we finished, we headed back to Shane's room which was different from his old hospital room since it was his own room. On the walls, were pictures that Ella colored taped up on the walls near the bed. Shane maneuvered his walker to an empty spot on his wall next to his bed then scotched taped the picture to the wall. A male nurse walked into the room and looked to Shane.

"Mr. Avis would you like a photograph of your family?" he asked.

"Sure, Paul thanks for asking," Shane said as he handed his phone to Paul.

Shane maneuvered his walker than stood by me then what really surprised me, he slipped his right arm around my waist in an affectionate embrace. Ella was in front with both of our hands on her shoulders.

"Smile," Paul said as he took the picture with the phone.

It felt good with his arm around me but then Shane let go and sat on the bed, Paul gave him his phone back. Paul left the room and Shane opened the picture to show us and we looked like a real family.

"Nice photo," Shane said.

I smiled at him. "Yes, it's a pretty nice-looking group of people there. We need to get going Shane, still have some more packing to do."

"I understand, it's exciting, only about 2 more weeks before I get out of here," Shane said. "And be able to get in our new home,"

Shane stood up with using his arms and gave both of us a hug and a kiss on the cheek that surprised me. It gave me an electric shock; I knew I wanted more but I resisted.

"I will see you on Saturday next week?" Shane asked.

I nodded. "We will both be there, maybe playing some chutes and Ladders?"

I looked down at Ella to emphasize.

"That sounds great momma," Ella said. "See you later Papa."

Ella took off running for the van so I waved to Shane and chased after her to catch up so I could open the doors. I got into the car and started it up then got a She-Ra cartoon going for Ella in the back of the van to watch. We drove in silence for at least a half hour until Ella asked a question.

"Momma, you like Shane a lot don't you," Ella asked.

I looked in the rear view mirror a second." Yes, I do Ella, but I will be getting paid to help Shane. We are not dating or married, you know that Ella, right?"

"I know momma but that's a bonus, right? Getting paid to like someone," Ella said.

I smiled. "Your right Ella, it's a bonus."

It took about another fifteen minutes till we got to our little driveway next to the mobile home and I parked. I got out and got Ella out of the van then locked it up before we headed inside into the mobile home. When we got inside, it was pretty bare now, we had our tv still with two lawn chairs in front of it and of course our beds. There were a few boxes in the living room and of course the rooms we slept in but we were ready to move. A neighbor down the block would be taking the beds the day before we leave. In a way I was really excited to be moving with Shane, he was a fighter but had a gentle spirit. A person who always wanted to do fun stuff and be there for his family. I started dinner since it was about 4:30 pm, I made hamburger helper, something called taco delight, it was really looking good. Ella must have come from her bedroom in her pajamas and She-Ra plushie doll in her arms. I dished the food on two paper plates and handed one to Ella.

"Let's go see what's on tv ok," I said.

We got settled into our lawn chairs then turned the tv on to watch some power puff girls and started eating our food. While I was eating, my phone vibrated and a message appeared on the screen from Shane. It was the photo we took of ourselves before we had left Shane's room, I nudged Ella and showed he the photo.

"Look at that, just like a real family," I said.

Ella giggled. "Can I get one?"

"I will forward it to my laptop and use the printer to print it out for you Ella," I said.

"Thank you, Momma," Ella said.

While she watched the tv I went to the laptop that sat on a kitchen counter and the printer that next to it. I opened the laptop powering it up then I forwarded the photo to my email so I could go to my email on the computer. I opened it up then made it into a decent sized photo for printing for Ella. It printed out then I went back over to Ella and gave her the photo so we could get back to eating. I changed the channel to our Disney plus and put a movie on, Race to Witch Mountain with Dwayne "The Rock" Johnson. I figured a few movies then off to bed with Ella so I could go into my room and relax so I could get to sleep. I knew there wasn't any school really since it was the end of May, creeping into June. Plus, I was done with regular work, now I was just packing and getting rid of stuff before the move. It has officially been 5 months since Shane's accident he would finally be getting out in 2 weeks from the recovery center. After watching a superhero movie on Disney, I switched off the tv.

"Let's get ready for bed Ella, I have a long day tomorrow," I said.

"Ok, Momma," Ella said.

I tucked her in bed and gave her a kiss on her forehead. "Night, Ella."

"Goodnight, Momma," Ella said then pull the blanket over her head.

I went into my room and actually got naked sine it was pretty hot in my room, even with 2 fans running. I laid on top of my bed then looked at the photo of Shane in his boxing trunks, sweating, he had signed the photo for me, with Love Shane at the end. I smiled and imagined Shane with his strong arms around me in bed. I truly enjoyed hanging out with Shane and he was really affectionate guy for Ella. I knew in my heart the move would bring us closer together as a family. I sent a text message to Shane.

Courtney: Have a good night, Shane.

Chapter Nine

Shane

I was still awake watching TV on ESPN, some actual boxing, when I received a text message from Courtney. I typed back a reply.

Courtney: Have a good night, Shane.

Shane: Have a good night, Courtney and God bless. I miss you.

I started to get up and stand near the wall by the tv then do wall pushups while watching a few of the fights. I was really getting excited for trying to get out of the recovery center and being in my own place since I still had an exercise bike, with a walking machine. I would hopefully get rid of the foot drop that was occurring from being in a coma so long. I knew it might hinder my return to the boxing ring if I could not fix it. I started doing some stretches and tried to massage the left ankle. I did that until I was tired and I dropped off into sleep.

The rest of the week went pretty fast with making them use the weight room more for different exercises to get me walking better. My father during the week, had dropped off some clothes for me and a walker that had wheels and brakes. I could tell my body was healing better since I could finally go to the bathroom normally by myself, bowel movements and Urinating. I looked at the family photo of me, Courtney and Ella smiling in the room. It gave me inspiration to try and get whole again so I could actually do family things. I prayed to God for forgiveness since I failed my first family and was falling in love with Courtney. It hurt my heart since once in a while I would look at the family photo of me, Christine and Tristan. I would cry every time I looked at the picture. I prayed for a normal life again, not as fancy or expensive, how I used to be with my money, more conservative. Plus, I used to drink a little heavier back when I did have money but I had slowed down once I had Tristan. I still drank so that was not good for my body so now I just worry about training and being a family man. I continued making sure doing the studying and physical therapy that the recovery center was giving me. Saturday had finally come and I waited outside for Courtney to come walking to the entrance of the building. I could see little Ella, wearing her jean shorts and a Powerpuff Girls T-shirt, carrying her She-Ra plushie doll. She was holding Courtney's hand as they walked through the parking lot. Courtney wore snug Jean shorts with a tank top that almost didn't fit her breasts, short socks, and tennis shoes. Ella ran up and gave me a hug then I hugged Courtney, kissed her on the cheek.

"Glad you guys could make it," I said.

Courtney kind of felt uncomfortable from the kiss on the cheek, especially since I knew I would be a future employer, not husband. I tried to remedy the situation quickly.

"Wow, one more week and I can get out of this joint," I said. "It will be a miracle."

"Will the new house be bigger than a mobile home, papa? "Ella asked.

"Yes, Ella but one floor and it has three bedrooms, a huge kitchen, with a nice size living room, "I said. "I can show you with my phone what it looks like."

I looked over at Courtney and smiled. " Like my new wheels?"

"Not bad, better than the walker from the hospital for sure," Courtney said.

"OK, we better head down and get some food, my little She-Ra needs to eat," I said.

We started down few hallways until we got to the rec room where they served lunch to the patients. We got a table and sat closest to the boardgames where they sat on a bookshelf, I grabbed the UNO cards. I then opened up my phone, with

Ella catching a glimpse of the picture of all of us, she giggled. Courtney smiled at me, I took that as a good sign then I went on the internet and found the website that was virtually showing the house. It was a green pre-fab home with a ramp in front and a nice driveway, plus storage shed. Inside was the living room right away, pretty decent sized than the kitchen, the bedrooms were not too small.

My father made sure it already had furniture with a nice sized table in the dining room which was right next to the living room. It had my 50-inch tv with a couch, recliner and coffee table, with an extra recliner on the side of the couch. When I showed the rooms, Ella's had everything Lightning McQueen in it with a race car bed. A few posters of She-Ra were up, with a cut out stand up near a wall of She-Ra. My room just consisted of a full- sized bed, Dresser, closet, and some exercise equipment. I had a walking machine that folded up against the wall and a nice exercise bike. A speedbag and heavy-bag were in the corner of my room. The main bedroom had a nice Queen- sized bed with floral bedspread and pillows, a dresser, closet and a nightstand. I looked over at Courtney.

"The main bedroom is yours Courtney so how does it look," I asked.

Courtney almost looked in tears and moved closer to me to give me a hug, even Ella gave me a hug.

"It looks wonderful Shane," Courtney said.

"I like my room the best," Ella said proudly.

I smiled. "I bet you do my little She-Ra, it's even better than mine."

The food we ordered with the kitchen workers arrived and we began to dig in, I actually got a cheeseburger and fries with a chocolate milk and water. I knew I was still pretty skinny since I went from 160 pounds to 113 pounds in a month from laying in a coma. I knew I had to keep eating healthy but some junk food to put meat back on my bones so I can get back to my normal weight for fighting. We ate in silence for a little while then gave our trays to the kitchen orderlies. I grabbed the deck of UNO cards and started shuffling the deck then gave everyone seven cards. I set up the first card to start matching.

"I haven't played this forever, has Ella played UNO?" I asked.

"No, this would be the first time," Courtney said.

"OK, Ella, this game is simple, just match the color or numbers," I said. "And you try to get rid of all of your cards to say UNO."

"Got it," Ella said.

We played for awhile and I for some reason out of the blue, I took my hand and rubbed Courtney's back in affection. Surprisingly, Ella won one game then Courtney won one game, I won zilch. The third hand, I finally got rid of all of my cards to win one game, then I put the cards back in the box and I put it back on the shelf. Courtney, I and Ella walked back to my room so I could find my wallet. I grabbed it and gave Courtney an envelope with two thousand dollars in it.

"This is for this last week and next week ok, "I said. "I think before we go, we should go into a fast oil change service and do a once over on the van before the long drive."

Courtney nodded. "That sounds like a good idea and thank you for the money."

"You really are doing me the biggest favor in the world for taking me back to my hometown," I said. "I will use my credit card if we go get your vehicle done."

We headed back down the maze of hallways to get to the front entrance to get out to the parking lot of the center. I stopped in the front entrance and Ella turned around, hugging my waistline.

"I will see you next week my little She-Ra," I said. "We will have some fun in the new house."

I didn't let Courtney get to far away from I immediately gave her a hug and kiss on the cheek, my penis sprung into action with feeling her breasts on my chest.

"See you next week, Courtney," I said.

She blushed a little. "You have a good week Shane, ok, bye for now."

Courtney took Ella's right hand and began walking into the parking lot to go look for their Sliver van. I gave a small wave as they walked away then headed back in to do more exercise in my room. I started doing a lot of pushups on my wall then triceps pushups from the chair and a lot of them. I turned on the tv to distract me from the pain in my elbows as I did the exercise, it would be the only way I would get stronger. I must have lost track of time, when the nurse came into tell me supper would be ready in the rec room. I acknowledged her then stopped and went in the bathroom to wash my face and hands. I walked with my walker with a nurse to the rec room then sat down at a table. I ate my food in silence, looking out the big pane glass window that was basically a wall. I looked at the sin city of Vegas, where the street lights were beginning to turn on from the darkness. Once I finished my meal, the orderlies took the plate away and I went ahead down the hallway back to my room, I switched on the tv then sat on the bed watching a CSI tv show for a while. I texted Courtney.

Shane: Courtney, I really had a good time today, thank you.

I am a thirty-six-year-old man, feeling like a sixteen- or seventeen-year-old just texting his crush that made me feel weird. It was now four months since the accident happen and I was just now getting up walking, my body beginning to heal. I still couldn't tell if God was messing with me or giving me a second chance at life. It was the thing to ponder for the rest of the night until I fell into sleep.

Chapter Ten

Courtney

I laid in bed thinking about Shane, when he kept touching me then giving me a kiss on the cheek. I couldn't tell if he really wanted me until before I left when he hugged me, I could feel something poke me through the clothing so I must have gotten excited when we were close. I think I was hoping he would give me a real kiss since he treated me like a woman he loved. I knew he would wait longer and I think God would want that anyways. Shane was looking way better now more energy but still skinny, which was normal for coma victims. I was getting excited about the new house; it was bigger than the mobile home I was in now. I just wish I was sleeping with Shane so I could feel his arms around me, while I slept. I was just about to drift off into sleep when I got a text from Shane.

Shane: Courtney, I really had a good time today, thank you.

Courtney: Your welcome Shane.

I felt happy with the text from him, it was weird since I knew he was now my boss technically, I just hoped for more. I have been alone for four years since the death of Travis and Ella couldn't really consider him her father since all he did was gamble and do drugs. I hungered for Shane's attention since it was easily given and I could tell now he wants me. I prayed to God and said I would wait for Shane to be whole again before pursuing his love. I drifted off into sleep dreaming of Shane and Ella.

The next day me and Ella, finished packing her clothes and toys she was bringing with, sticking them in to the back of the van. I had gotten rid of a lot of clothes and kept the only ones I would really wear. I had four boxes and a small bag for shoes that I stuck in back of the van with two extra boxes of a few books, pictures, knick-Knacks. I let a couple of neighbors take the beds and I sold the tv, tv stand. It would be boring for a few days before we would go pick up Shane from the center. The morning of the pickup I put on a light blue V-neck t-shirt, blue jean shorts, short socks, tennis shoes and I made sure my legs were shaved. It was now the end of June by the time we went to go pick up Shane from the center, I'm sure he was really ready to get out of there. I pulled up into the parking lot then went into the pick-up area for the center by the front doors. Shane was standing with Lisa the blonde nurse by the front doors and his parents. He was wearing a Summerhill hospital t-shirt, blue jeans, with grey Sketcher tennis shoes.

He looked still skinny but his arms were getting their muscle tone back and he looked happy. He was shaking his father's hand then he gave his mother a hug. I stopped the van, opened the automatic side door then I got out to help Shane put his walker in the vehicle. I stopped to see Shane's mother who was pretty, aging elegantly with light brunette hair, summer dress on. His father looked like he was going to the beach with cargo shorts, sandals, Amsoil t-shirt. He was slightly taller than Shane at 6'0-foot, dark brown hair just starting to grey, goatee. Ella jumped out with her She-Ra t shirt on, jean shorts, tennis shoes, bounded for Shane and hugged his waistline.

"Papa!" Ella said.

I think it really struck a nerve on Shane's mother and father; they were taken back by Ella's affection for Shane. Plus, since they just lost their grandson in the accident, it might have hurt them. It didn't faze Shane and I swore I could see tears in his eyes as he knelt down and hugged little Ella.

"It's good to see you little She-Ra," Shane said.

I hurried to rectify the situation. "Ella, please get back in the van ok."

"Ok," Ella said and went back to get into her booster seat.

Shane turned to his parents. "You remember Courtney from the hospital, I hope. She will be helping me in Duluth, while I recover."

They both shook my hand. "I'm sorry about Ella, she really likes Shane."

Hope smiled." That's alright, my little boy turned out to be a good father so I understand why she likes him so much."

I smiled at Shane's mother. "Yes, he is, and a very generous employer."

"Well, I hope things go well for you and Shane," Don said. "I and Hope have to get to the grocery store so we will let you get going."

It felt kind of weird once his dad said that, like we were already dating or something but I brushed it off and took Shane's walker, folding it so it would go into the van. Shane held onto the front door and gave a small wave to his parents before getting into the passenger seat, he set his one bag on the other side of Ella. Shane looked over at me and smiled.

"Well let's stop at an oil change service then get something to eat than get on the road," Shane said.

I nodded. "Sounds like a good idea."

We got on the road and went near North of Las Vegas but to a Valvoline Oil change shop, where we had them do an oil change, transmission change, radiator flush. They also changed the wiper blades and air filter. Shane did not even blink an eye when came up to 600 dollars. He took out his credit card and paid them. My van was loving it because it seemed to run smoother after all the maintenance done to it. We went to a gas station with a McDonalds attached to it and ordered food after we fueled up. I turned on a movie in the back for Ella as she ate a happy meal of a cheeseburger and fries. We drove for awhile and got on I-90 East and stayed on it then Shane started talking to me.

"We should try to drive for at least 6 hours with breaks for gas then find a hotel once it's dark," Shane said.

"Ok, that should be fine," I said.

He looked over at me." What kind of movies do you like?"

"Lots of comedies, some action, fantasy, science fiction and sports," I said. "As a woman, I do like my romance movies once in a while."

"Wow, my kind of woman," Shane chuckled. "How about music?"

I smiled. "I like rock, pop and country, and R&B. How about you?"

"I like Rock, R&B, some country, some rap, dance music," Shane said." Some sort of tempo for training."

I smiled. "Something like Eye of the Tiger."

Shane chuckled. "Something like that."

"So, you grew up in Duluth then?" I asked.

Shane nodded. "Yes, my father worked in real estate and my mom worked as a computer programmer for a company in there. They of course retired in Las Vegas."

"Do you love Duluth?" I asked.

Shane chuckled. "Not really, but my trainer lives there and he's like family. I do have an aunt and Uncle that still lives there, plus some cousins. Another Aunt just lives over the bridge in Superior, Wisconsin. I do not love Duluth since the winter storms sometimes really sucks."

"Well, if nothing else you can keep training so you can get back in shape and improve your walking," I said. "I love going for walks so if you don't mind, I will go with you sometimes."

Shane smiled. "I would like that, Courtney."

We had finished our food then drove for a couple of hours then stopped at another gas station to fill up and get rid of the garbage. Shane handed me the credit card and I got out of the van, he slipped out his door. I went to the other side where the gas pump was and used the credit card then started pumping gas. I saw Shane on the other side trying to stretch his legs then he opened the side door for Ella. She jumped out of the vehicle and gave Shane a hug again which brought a smile to my face. I finished pumping gas and put the handle back into its cradle, I saw Ella take Shane's hand. He began walking over to me slowly, his left foot dragging slightly as he approached.

"Please be careful Shane," I said.

He smiled. "I will, I have both of you nearby, just don't speed walk away from me ok."

"I won't," I said.

I went on the other side of Shane and took his other hand, we headed into the Holiday gas station together. I helped Shane get to the men's bathroom then I took Ella into the Ladies bathroom. I am sure Shane used the wall for support so I wasn't too worried just when he was out in the gas station parking lot. We all got done, I washed my hands with Ella then went back into the store to get a drink. I paid for the drinks which were mostly diet pop since I didn't like the sugar for Ella. I instantly took Shane's hand and so did Ella then we helped him walk back to the van. He turned to me before we opened the door.

"Thank you, Courtney," Shane said.

"You're welcome," I said.

I helped put little Ella back into her booster seat, buckling her in then inserted another Disney movie into the player, The Incredibles. I got back into the van and started it up then we took off down the road again. Shane looked over at me.

"So, you said you are from Iowa?" Shane asked.

“I was born in Nebraska and moved to Iowa when I was six years old,” I said. “My father had bought a farm there so I am a farmer’s daughter.”

“That’s good to know,’ he said.

Shane turned on the radio and put an oldies station on.” That ok”.

‘Sure,” I said.

We sat listening to the radio for 3 hours and checking the scenery since we must have pulled into Wyoming once it was getting dark. I found a small hotel off the highway and we pulled next to the check in. Shane got out and did his stretches again while I got out to go with him into the check in with Ella in tow. A tall man with a beard was standing behind a counter, once we walked in, giving us a nice greeting.

“Howdy folks, you need a room for the night, with two beds?” he asked.

“Yes, if it’s possible,” Shane said then he turned his head. “That ok Courtney?”

I must have been in a daze since I just blurted out. “Sure.”

Shane handed the man his credit card then the man ran it through his card reader then pulled a slip for Shane to sign. He signed the paper then he put the plates and the vehicle info for the man behind the counter. He then gave Shane a key card for a door.

“I do have cameras watching the parking lot so if anything happens, we will know about it,” The man said. “It’s pretty safe here, room 113.”

“Thank you,” Shane said.

We got back into the van then parked in front of the hotel room since it’s only one floor, Shane grabbed his bag. I went and got Ella out then I grabbed a bag for the two of us I made up for the hotel stays. We locked up the vehicle and Shane opened up the hotel room door. Inside it had the normal look with two beds and 2-night stands, big dresser with TV on it, a small table and 2 chairs then a bathroom. I went to the bathroom first, taking a quick shower then dressing in blue gym shorts.

"The shower does have a shower bar so you can keep yourself steady," I said. "Or do you want me to help you?'

Shane blushed. "I should be good thanks for asking though, I will take a quick shower too."

Shane went in a little slower but he looked steady enough to get it done as he went into the bathroom. Ella changed into her pajamas while Shane showered and I turned on the TV to find a show to watch.

Chapter Nine

Shane

I went into the bathroom carrying a white t-shirt and grey pajama pants then got into the shower. I used a rag from the hotel and soap to clean up, holding onto the shower bar inside the shower stall. I felt cleaner then took my folded clothes with shoes in the other room and set them on the dresser. Courtney sat on one bed and Ella on the other watching the big bang theory on tv.

"Did you want me to sleep on the floor?" I asked.

Courtney patted the bed she was on. " No, you can sleep on this bed, it's big enough for both of us."

I sat down next to her, I was really surprised since I thought she would sleep with Ella in her bed, maybe I did have a chance with her. After the one episode, Courtney found Futurama on the comedy station.

"I'm sorry I can't really drive yet," I said. "I just feel unsafe with my left foot."

"That's ok Shane," Courtney said.

I smiled. "I was thinking, when we go through the cities can we stop at the Mega mall."

"Sure, if you want to," Courtney said.

"All of my old clothes don't fit so," I said. "I need a few more jeans and shirts. Plus, I want to take Ella through the aquarium and the Nickelodeon Park."

Ella jumped up then came rushing at me then giving me a hug." You really mean it."

"Yes, my little She-Ra," I said, hugging her back.

"If that's what you really want," Courtney said.

"I do," I said.

We all three sat in the bed watching two more episodes of Futurama then I helped Ella into bed tucking her in then kissing her forehead. Courtney also gave her a kiss good night, then she squeezed my hand pulling me over to the bed. I got under the covers; Courtney shut out the lights then laid on her side with her butt up against my penis. I felt embarrassed that I had a hard erection but I snuggled up, holding my angel then I fell into a blissful sleep smelling the Lavender still on her skin. I moved around in my sleep once in a while but would go back to my normal position of cuddling with Courtney. I woke up six AM since I had to go the bathroom then I began stretching on the floor, trying not to make to much noise. I started doing pushups on my knees since my left foot was so weak. I got at least twenty in then started doing sit-ups, my grunting must of woke up Courtney so she got up. I smiled at her as I did crunches as she stretched out then looked at me.

"Good morning, Courtney," I said.

She smiled. "Good morning, Shane,"

Courtney went over and shook Ella lightly to wake her up then handed her some clothes to put on in the bathroom. I finished my exercises then continued to stretch and try to stretch the left ankle so my calf muscle would relax. I turned my body over to the bed then used my arms to push myself up. Courtney was taking out a few articles of clothing out of her bag to go change into.

"You look like you're getting better getting off the ground, Shane," Courtney said.

"I am starting to feel better," I said. "I think it will be 3 more months before I can start training for boxing again.

"Well, be patient for now and just keep working your body," Courtney said then went into the bathroom. Ella came springing out and hugged me again so I tickled her then gave her a kiss on her forehead.

"Morning, little She-Ra, ready for more of a long drive?' I asked. "And some adventure."

"I am papa," Ella said.

Every-time she called me that it melted my heart and almost would bring me to tears but I would give a sad smile and hug her again Courtney came out with a lowcut V-neck t-shirt white with cargo shorts and tennis shoes. She looked really hot with her long brunette hair in a pony tail. My mouth was open too long, probably I was drooling, looking at her.

"Something wrong, Shane?" Courtney asked.

I caught myself. "Mm, no just getting a little extra air. I have an idea since we will be running through South Dakota."

She smiled. "What is it?"

"We should pit stop at the black hills and get some shots on our phones and the wall, plus Sioux Falls, south Dakota," I said. "It's on the way."

She finished repacking her bags the way she wanted it then turned back to me.

"If that's what you want to do, it's a great idea since Ella has not seen much," Courtney said. "I never got the chance to give her a vacation ever."

I hurried and surprised her with a hug so I could feel her big breasts on me then a kiss on her cheek.

"Then I guess we will be giving Ella great time then," I said.

I was silently praying to God I could hold off from practically mauling Courtney since I knew in my heart, I did love this woman. I think I wanted her more since she excepted me for who I was even if I was broken. I wanted to spend what days left on earth with Courtney there was no doubt in my mind, I needed her as my wife. We got our bags and Courtney stayed on my right side holding my arm to help steady my walk since my balance was still off. I threw both the bags in and helped buckle Ella in while Courtney dropped the key card off. I found the Incredibles 2 movie and stuck it into the DVD player, kissed Ella's forehead again.

"Alright, we should be on the road shortly, Ella," I said.

Courtney came out of the office then walked over to the van and got into the driver seat. We drove to the nearest gas station which was Speedway and fueled up. I listened to music for a few hours and just looked out, watching the scenery. Courtney spoke, breaking my trance from the window.

"What are you thinking about?" Courtney asked.

"I'm thinking I am the luckiest man on earth," I said not looking at her. "I survived almost dying and I get to see such a beautiful landscape with two people I want to be with."

I heard a sharp intake of breath at that." I guess I am really grateful I am alive, I beat the knockout of death. I don't mean to make you feel uncomfortable Courtney."

"Don't worry, I think I know what you mean Shane," Courtney said.

I turned and gave a sad smile. "We crossed over to South Dakota right, I hope we make the Black Hills by at least one."

"I think we will," Courtney said.

She ended up being right since it was a 4-hour drive but we got there, fueled up again then stopped checked out the sights in numerous areas, getting out of the van to do it. We at least messed around for about an hour there, telling Ella about the Indian history. We got back on the road; I was looking at photos of my phone we took and some that a couple had helped to take of us as a family again. I showed a few to both Courtney and Ella as we drove down I-90 again. It was just starting to get dark, when we pulled into Wall, South Dakota, it looked like an old Western town. We parked and went into a few shops so I could get a few T-shirts for them and me. I found one pair of jeans that was only 45 bucks, luckily and found a cool stuffed animal for Ella, necklace for Courtney. After walking around and checking sights we found a diner and had supper together. While we were eating, I spoke to Courtney.

“There’s a Best Western close by that we can stay for the night,” I said.

“Ok, if we can afford it,” Courtney said.

“We will be fine,” I said.

After dinner, we took Ella over by a mechanical horse and let her ride it for a while, taking pictures of her laughing, smiling. We drove over to the Best Western and got another room so we could rest for the night. Courtney allowed me again to just get a room with two beds and we would be sharing one bed together again. I went first and changed into my pajamas in the bathroom then watched some cartoons with Ella. She got close and cuddled me while watching then Courtney came out wearing her gym shorts. She sat down with I and Ella then cuddled both of us. I think that was the happiest time of my life, God was being gracious and giving me a life with two loving people. I cried right then and there, tears rolling down my eyes as I held both of them. Courtney kissed my left cheek then continued to hold me as we watched Sponge Bob on tv. We watched a few more shows together, surprisingly, Futurama then we shut out the lights and this time, Courtney grabbed my arm and put my hand on her breast as we cuddled. I instantly fell asleep smelling the Lavender on her neck.

Chapter Twelve

Courtney

I felt Shane's arms around me and his lips against my neck as we lay in the darkness together. I wanted this man badly to want me, I knew he was holding back so the cuddling was as good as I would get for now. I enjoyed this semi vacation with Ella and Shane, I hadn't done anything this fun since I was a teenager. God had answered my prayers to finally meeting such a compassionate man, who was a real family man. I slept so soundly with Shane's arms wrapped around me and I knew he wasn't shallow since I was not a skinny model like the last one, he had. He was definitely getting better and stronger every day. I woke up to the sounds of some grunting again as I saw Shane doing Knee pushups next to the bed. I smiled down at him.

"Hey, Tarzan, how you feeling?" I spoke.

"Great, I am ready for our next trip to Sioux Falls," Shane said. "They have a cool park there so Ella can play. The sights are awesome there."

I got out of bed then crouched down and kissed Shane's cheek which surprised him but then he smiled. I took my clothes that I was going to wear for the day and went into the bathroom to take a shower. I showered off then dried off, putting an Undertaker tank top with my jean shorts and tennis shoes. I made sure my legs were shaven with my Vagina area clean also since a lot of hair bothered me while I showered. I sprayed some of my Lavender perfume on me then put it in my travel bag. I went out and stuck my stuff in the big duffel bag with clothes in it while Shane was stretching his legs and ankles. I shook Ella awake.

"Ella, it's time to get up and get a move on so we can keep driving," I said.

Shane was getting up and taking a few clean clothes that he bought then brought it in with him into the bathroom. Ella got up groggily as I helped change her into clean clothes then brushed her hair and put it in a pony tail. Shane came out of the bathroom, looking cleaned and refreshed in his Mount Rushmore t-shirt and wearing skinny jeans which fit him. He looked at me then looked shocked.

"Oh my god! You are my kind of woman," Shane said.

I laughed. "You are crazy and yes I do like the Undertaker."

"Wow, that's great! If they have some pro wrestling in Duluth, I am taking you," Shane said.

I could tell he couldn't stop looking at my breasts which is why I wore the tank top to begin with so he could enjoy looking at me. I looked at my watch it was getting to seven so I knew we better get moving, it was now Saturday. I am hoping we get to the new place by Monday or Tuesday to get situated. I took Ella in the bathroom to make her brush her teeth and wash her face. We stepped out and looked to Shane.

"Well, we better get moving," I said.

Shane picked up his duffel bag. "Let's go."

I grabbed our bag then walked to the van to unlock it so Shane could buckle in Ella and put the bags in while I got rid of the room key. I came out after I dropped it off and could see Shane had finished buckling in Ella then kiss her forehead. While I got closer, he got a movie into the DVD player in the back for Ella. I could see Shane tickle Ella and she was laughing as I came up to Shane.

"The tickle monster has you!!" Shane said.

Ella laughed. "Stop the monster mommy!"

I smiled then tugged on Shane's arm." Alright, tickle monster, let's get the show on the road."

Shane smiled and closed the side door of the van then he kissed me on the cheek. "Ready."

Shane got into the passenger side while I got into the driver side of the van then I started it up, heading to the nearest gas station to fill up. We filled up and got some snacks for the trip then started driving down I-90 again. It took us about 4 more hours to get to Sioux Falls, South Dakota. I thought it just looked like just another town until Shane directed me to the falls in town. We parked the car with Ella jumping out right away, ready to check everything out, the falls were beautiful. Shane got to the left side of me and took my hand, I'm sure for balance, maybe for me, I couldn't tell. I knew he wanted to try and stay professional with me but I could tell he also desired me. This was another family outing and it was fun and wondrous with the sights. There was a small playground near the falls so I knew that we would let Ella run around to tire herself out. We were walking up a stairway of like a tower to view the falls better and it was definitely exercise for Shane climbing the stairs for his foot. A couple that was looking out at the falls asked if we wanted a picture of ourselves. We had Ella Stand in front of us, Shane had his arm around my waist and smiled for the picture. Two thirty-six-year-olds smiling like teenage love crushes. I helped Shane go down the stairs after checking out the falls and led him to picnic table near the jungle gym kiddie park. We sat down together, watching little Ella play with a couple of other kids while Shane had his hand on my left leg.

"So, what do you think?" Shane asked. "You enjoying yourself?"

"Oh my god, yes Shane," Courtney said. "Plus, Ella will be loving you more now. You will be her permanent papa."

"I am enjoying this myself; I haven't had a vacation for about 2 years actually. I was training too much to become a contender."

"Wow, that's crazy," I said.

"I know, this has been the best 2 days so far," Shane leaned in close. "Courtney, I think you're really beautiful."

Shane was about to kiss me when Ella came screaming in and hugged me then Shane.

"We better get going," Shane said.

I nodded then got up and helped walk with him to the van, getting him to the passenger door. I helped buckle Ella into her booster seat then got another cartoon movie into the DVD player. I jumped into the driver seat and got back on the road going towards Minnesota. We sat in silence for awhile then I took a glance back at Ella and she was out cold.

"That must have really tired her out," I said.

Shane turned to me." I'm sorry about before, that was really unprofessional of me trying to try and kiss you."

"That's ok but I think if you're having second thoughts, you should let me know," I said.

"I'm not having second thoughts, I am having family thoughts," Shane said. "But I want to be whole before trying to be with you."

"Ok, I think I understand and I am on the same page with you," I said. "Ever since I have met you from the hospital, I can't stop thinking about you."

Shane smiled. "I can't stop thinking about you either. I just want to take this slow. I know you want your career. I still want your help and will pay every 2 weeks like I said."

I glanced over at him. "That sounds about right, once we get to the house, we get things straightened out."

"Alright, boss," Shane said with a grin.

It took us another 4 and half hours to get into the cities so we could get to the Mall of America, switching roads using the GPS on my phone. We parked near the hotel that was connected to the shopping mall and in the parking ramp. I took a disability parking spot. I put up the sign that was given from Shane's father. I rummaged through a box in the back of the van, getting a swimsuit for me and Ella. Shane grabbed his walker this time, putting his bag on the chair part of the wheeled walker. I closed the back of the van then locked it; we went into the ramp elevator getting to the floor we needed to cross to get there. We entered Radisson Blu and checked into the hotel. We all used the bathroom then we went into the mall and began walking around. Shane insisted we stop in the Nickelodeon Park so both he and Ella could go on some Kiddy rides. We also checked out the Malls aquarium which was fun for Ella and me, I loved looking at all the fish, sharks. We had to stop at the Old Navy so Shane could get some more jeans and t-shirts, underwear, socks that fit his skinny ripped frame. After all the fun we had supper at the food court at Jonny Rocket.

I helped Shane carry some of his bags back to the hotel room that didn't fit in his chair. We settled down in our room watching the Disney channel on cable for Ella. Shane sat close to me, with his arm around my waist as we watched the show the Simpsons. Ella sat close in front of us on the same bed. I really enjoyed the closeness of Shane. Once in a while, he would touch my hair, running his hands through it. I was scared I might attack him, while Ella was there, but I held back just enjoying his touch. We got tired then we all changed in our pajamas and Shane did his ritual of tucking Ella in for bedtime. He kissed her forehead then got in bed with me, instantly cuddling my body. I shut off the light and let the darkness take me. In the night Shane had to adjust because of his calf muscle was bothering him so we would switch and I would put my arm around his waist. The morning came fast and I felt like something brushed my lips and right cheek. I heard some grunting on the floor next to the bed so I knew Shane was stretching and exercising again. I got the covers off of me and stretched out with a yawn, glancing at Shane exercising.

"You sleep alright?' I asked him.

Shane smiled. "Like a baby. You, ok?"

"Yes, I better get a shower in then I want to take Ella to the pool for a while," I said.

"Sounds good, I will probably shower and come down to watch you guys before we get out of here," Shane said.

Shane was doing his pushups while I went and showered, changed into a one- piece swim suit then put my hair in a pony tail. I got out then Shane went in with his new clothes he bought to go shower and change. I woke up Ella and got her into her one-piece swimsuit she had with her, putting her long brunette hair in a pony tail. Shane got out, we were holding our towels and ready to go, he followed me, looping his arm into mine. The pool was crazy, had at least 3 slides, a lazy man river and a kiddie area that Ella loved. Shane sat at a table by himself watching us and taking pictures. We stayed until 9:30 in the morning so about an hour, then we headed back to the room to change. Shane got his duffel bag ready and stuffed all of his new clothes in while we changed in the bathroom. We dropped the key card at the front desk then had some complimentary breakfast they had there. The whole week was my first vacation in a longtime and I had enjoyed being with Shane the whole time. Ella could not get enough of him, always giving him a hug. I guided us back to the van, unlocking it with my key fob then Shane got Ella into her booster seat. He buckled her in then grabbed a Disney movie, The Beauty and the Beast, putting it in the DVD player. I got in the driver seat, starting up the van, while Shane jumped into the passenger side.

"Well, this should be the home stretch," Shane said. "I checked the weather it's not going to fun getting there, a storm is brewing."

“I’ll be extra careful then,” I said with a smile.

The drive going North was ok going past Forest Lake then the rain, lightning, thunder started happening and I could see Shane begin to panic.

Chapter Thirteen

Shane

The Lightning, thunder and the down pouring rain all of a sudden started giving me flashbacks of the terrible accident. I felt my throat closing up and I couldn't breathe, tears streamed down my eyes.

"Stop the car!" I yelled. "Please stop the car."

Courtney turned and went under a bridge for the highway to put in park with the flashers on.

"Shane, breathe please," Courtney said rubbing my back. "It's ok, we're stopped. We're alright."

I don't know, out of foolishness or just being plain scared, I took Courtney's face in my hands pulling her to my lips. It felt like a shock to my system, probably which I needed, with a long kiss that both left us breathless. Ella giggled in the back so after a few moments I stopped, touching Courtney's hair before I backed into my chair. Ella touched my shoulder from the back.

"I'm sorry Courtney," I said. "I think I was having a flashback; I might have PTSD from the accident."

Courtney cleared her throat. "That's ok Shane. I understand, we can stay here until the rain settles down ok."

I looked over at her and she turned, giving me her Angelic smile, which made me want her more. It relieved whatever anxiety I was having from the storm.

"Ok that's a good idea," I said.

We waited until the rain became just a normal light rainfall then got back on I-35, heading North to Duluth. It took us a good three hours to get to the Duluth, I was glad the rain let up so we wouldn't have any more issues. We stayed on 35 going into town, it was a sight to see as the Lake and the city off the skyline look out, we had to get to Trinity Road near the Mall entrance. I gave Courtney the address so she could put it in her GPS for the phone and we could find the new house. My father had texted me and said he had someone fill the freezers with food and the cabinets. I was really thankful he did that so I wouldn't have to go shopping for 2 weeks. Everything was set-up and ready to go, he even texted me the combination to a box in the front that had the house keys. Courtney pulled into the big driveway, next to the Green pre fab home, storage shed. I could see the wooden ramp that was to the front door. It also was a small deck so you could sit outside in the summer. In the very small front lawn was a firepit, the rest was just dirt and rock driveway.

"It looks nice for a small house," I said glancing at Courtney.

"It sure does," Courtney said.

She jumped out the door and went to the back grabbing my walker for me so I could put my duffel bag on it.

"I will drop this off and we can bring some more boxes in on my little walker," I said.

Courtney nodded and I rolled up the ramp with my walker then I found the small key box right next to the front door. I punched in the numbers and the box opened so I could grab the keys to the house, I unlocked the front door. I opened it then tossed my duffel bag into the dining room area. I hurried back over to them and grabbed the duffel bag Courtney was using and rolled up the ramp to the front door. I tossed that one in the dining room then was about to go grab some more stuff, when I almost ran into Courtney. I gave her another kiss lightly on the lips since she had her hands full. It surprised her but she smiled then I went and grabbed a box from Ella so she wouldn't struggle with it since it was heavier than normal. I rolled it up and put it in the dining room area with the bags. Courtney had thrown her clothes in big garbage bags so it was easier to store in the van. I helped bring all the clothes in for Ella and Courtney while Courtney did the boxes. There was about 5 total since she got rid of or sold most of her stuff since this place was already furnished with almost everything. Once we finished, we went inside to get a real good look at the inside of the house. I sat down in a dining chair with a nice sized wooden table. In the living room, was a couch and a recliner with a coffee table, a 50-inch TV on the wall near the big front window.

“What do you think? “I asked.

“It’s great! Can I check my room?” Ella asked.

I smiled. “Sure, Ella.”

I stood up and then grabbed my duffel bag, dragging it back to my room so I didn’t have to use the walker to get back there. My room was smaller than the other two bedrooms, I just had a single bed, dresser, closet, exercise bike and a running machine that folded up against the wall. I laid the duffel bag on my bed and took the dirty clothes out of the bag, putting them in a laundry basket next to the foot of the bed. I texted my father and asked him if I had cable or not, he massaged back saying he put Sling in since it was cheaper. The internet was installed on the TV, the box sitting on a stand next to the TV. I thanked him again then Courtney stopped by my room.

“I put a pizza in the oven since it was already in the freezer,” Courtney said. “There is a box freezer next to the kitchen counter which has more food in it. They really stocked it up for us.”

“Nice,” I said. “I have been thanking my dad three times already. He really came through for me.”

I followed Courtney over to Ella’s room where she was playing with a He-Man, She-Ra by Castle Gray skull and Snake Mountain.

There were a few more old action figures of Man at arms, Teela, Orko and Prince Adam. Some bad guys like Evil Lynn were there and Skeletor were next to Snake Mountain. I could tell it used to be my toys when I was kid. Tristan's old racing bed was in the room and stand up of Lightning McQueen was up against a wall. The toys were set on a small bookshelf, next to a Lightning McQueen dresser.

"You like it, Ella?" I asked.

Ella stopped playing and ran to me hugging my waist. "I love it papa!"

I kneeled down and properly hugged her then kissed her forehead. "I'm glad."

"Let's go get some pizza!" Courtney said.

We walked back into the dining room where Courtney had moved the boxes in an orderly fashion so we could sit at the table. The TV was already going since Courtney must have figured out the controllers, it was on the Disney channel. She had cut up the pizza in squares and placed them on plates already in different spots. The table had four chairs and was a decent sized square table. There was even a dart board put up in the living room on a side wall with the darts in it. We sat down in a spot where there was a plate in front of us and a can of diet cola.

"Can I make a prayer?" Ella asked.

I smiled. "Sure, little She-Ra. What you going to pray for?"

Ella giggled. "You'll see."

Courtney then Ella grabbed hands then me, I was excited to be touching Courtney's soft hands as Ella began to pray.

"Thank you, God, for giving me a papa again and I thank you for the house and family," Ella said.

I could feel the tears well up in my eyes as I smiled at Ella. "Thank you, Ella."

We let go then started eating pizza. "Tomorrow, if you can help me get to the shed to check out the snow blower, that would be good."

"No problem, Shane," Courtney said touching my hand.

I really wanted to jump her bones but I felt I needed to hold off longer to train my body to move better before trying anything. I smiled at her.

"The next week, I think if you owe anything on your van, I should pay it off so you just have to worry about insurance," I said. "Plus, you will be able to save more money then."

"I only owe two thousand left on it" Courtney said. "That would be a big relief."

"Also, I need to get to the clinic for a fitting for a prosthetic for my left foot, this Thursday, if you can drive me," I said.

"I will put it on the calendar," Courtney said.

"Thank you," I said then went back to eating pizza.

We watching some sort of cartoon called American Dragon: Jake Long together while we ate pizza. Ella would giggle at the cartoon, now and again or I would tickle her sporadically making her laugh. Once we got done eating food, I went to finish putting away my clothes and look in the closet to see what I had. I found one of my boardgames my father bought me as a kid, Quest for the Dungeon Master from the cartoon. I brought it out since it was like Candyland in a way so it would be easy for Ella to play. I brought it to the table and set it up then looked for them. Courtney was just finishing up hanging up clean clothes in the main room, when I knocked on her open door.

"Hey, I found a game to play if your interested?" I spoke.

Courtney stopped and smiled. "Sure, let's go get Ella."

We walked over to her new room, where she was just playing with her action figures again, using Skeletor fighting She-Ra, trying to make special effects with her mouth.

"Want to play a fun game, Ella?" I asked.

Ella stopped then got up and ran to me, grabbing my hand then tugging me along to go back to the dining room. We sat down at the table then grabbed our character tabs for the board and put it on the beginning spot. It was already about six PM at night when we started playing and when we finished it was after eight. I could tell they both enjoyed it, like usual it made me very happy. I was glad I wasn't really in training for a fight then I would have less time with my new family. Officially, it now had been five months since the accident, I needed to move on, Christine's parents hated me, blamed me for her and Tristan's death. Which of course wasn't totally true since the Trucker wasn't watching where he was driving that night. I finally felt healed in my soul, not angry or as sad I was in the first two months. Ella won one game then Courtney got to the Dungeon Master. I helped put the boardgame away then we all watched a Futurama show on one of the Sling channels. We all sat on the couch, I actually had my arm around Courtney's shoulders while Ella laid on her mother's lap. Once the show finished, Courtney helped get Ella ready for bed and then I made sure to tuck her in, kissing her forehead.

"Goodnight, little She-Ra," I said.

Courtney gave Ella a kiss goodnight also then proceeded to head to her room and I followed behind. Courtney turned around.

"May I kiss you goodnight," I said. "I think you know I am in love with you but I do want to wait before dating you steady. I want to be more healed."

Courtney smiled. "I know and I agree with what you wish to do. Yes, you can kiss me goodnight."

I pulled her close in my arms then giving her a long and gentle kiss on the mouth. I could feel her soft breasts on my chest as I held her. I stepped back after the kiss was done, flustered.

"Goodnight, Courtney," I said.

"Goodnight, Shane, "she said.

She closed the door, then I went to my room so I could get undressed and relax in my new bed, I got under the covers after shutting the light off.

Chapter Fourteen

Courtney

I had got into my gym shorts after kissing Shane, it felt weird when he said the words, I love you, it made me feel all tingly all inside. I set the alarm from my phone so I could get up to finish putting stuff away. This new house or new beginning was my dream come true, to be with a person who would equally share my love for Ella. Two parents, not just a single mom anymore, he seemed like he would help around the house and be there for me. I laid in bed with my phone in hand and looked at the photos we did of each other for the past week. I literally felt happy and secure for the first time in my life, I knew our life would be good for us. I fell asleep dreaming of Shane putting his arms around me and cuddling. The sleep must have gone by fast; I felt my phone vibrating on my chest as the alarm went off. I got up and grabbed all my stuff out of the duffel bag putting dirty clothes into a laundry basket next to my bed. Shane's father really set this place up nice. The freezer food, there was canned goods, noodle side dishes, instant potatoes in the pantry or cabinets in the kitchen. The bedroom layout was good too, he really cared about his son. I went past Shane's bedroom so I could wake up Ella so I could make breakfast. He was riding his exercise bike and looked almost normal doing it, I peeked in knocked on his door so he could hear me. He was shirtless and looked sweaty, his body was becoming more muscle now then skinny, it really excited me to see his body was getting back to its old self. He smiled when he saw me.

"Good morning, Shane," I said. "I will be making pancakes with the pancake mix in the pantry. Would you be interested?"

"I definitely would, I need to gain all of my weight back somehow," Shane said.

"Ok, I will be working on it in a few minutes if you want to shower," I said.

I then walked down the hall to my daughter's room, where she was already playing with the toys that was given to her. I watched from the door for a few minutes just smiling as she tried making special effects for Skeletor and She-Ra as they fought. I cleared my throat.

"Ella, I will be making pancakes in a few minutes so get yourself dressed," I said.

She turned and smiled. "Ok mommy."

I walked to the kitchen and found all the stuff in the kitchen to make pancakes. Who ever did the shopping even left instant milk so I could use it to whip up the pancake mix with? I was whipping it in the bowl, when I felt Shane's arms around me from the back. I turned slightly and gave Shane a kiss on the lips.

"Good morning, Courtney," Shane said.

I felt almost week in the knees so I was glad I was in his arms, he smelled like he had just showered with a bar of soap. I could feel his manhood excited up against my rear as we kissed then he pulled away to go to the dining room. I started cooking them up and stacking them on a plate as Ella came running out to Shane when she saw him.

"Papa, good morning!" Ella said, giving him a hug.

Shane was wearing his pajama pants and a white t-shirt with tennis shoes, Ella in her She-Ra t-shirt, blue jeans, tennis shoes. I was assuming it was Shane's workout clothes for the moment and would probably do more exercise a little later. I must have stacked at least ten on the plate which I thought would be a good number if everyone had three or two pancakes. I found syrup in the cupboards and butter in the fridge. I brought the pancake plate to the table and the syrup, then went back for the butter. I grabbed that and brought it to the table as Shane tickled Ella, making her laugh. I smiled at that and set the plates, forks out on the table for everyone to use to get the pancakes. Ella jumped in to want to do another prayer so we held hands as she said her prayer.

"Thank you, God, for this food and family," Ella said.

"That's a nice prayer, Ella," Shane said.

We got to eating the pancakes with the syrup and butter and in silence for awhile then Shane spoke up.

"A little later, can we go get some more groceries?" Shane asked. "If that's ok, plus I need to go to the bank to withdraw some cash."

"Sure, that's fine, I was just going to empty my boxes in my room," I said.

We all ate three pancakes a piece and I really felt full after that, I'm sure Shane was about to explode since this was his first big meal in a while. Once everyone was done eating, I took the dirty dishes and set them in the sink to clean. I did them up while Shane and Ella went back to their rooms for a while. I also unpacked the rest of the boxes then broke them down and stuffed them in a recycle bin outside on the driveway. I saw next to it that there was also a trash bin that was just as big as the recycle bin. I was really impressed with Shane's father, he really got him set up again. It must have been close to or after noon since I saw Shane walking around in some Old Navy t-shirt and Jeans. He looked like he was getting his muscle tone and made him look sexier than he already was.

"You already to go?" I asked.

"Yes, but I expect you want to change before leaving, "Shane said.

I smiled. "Yes, your probably right."

I had found next to my room was sort of a divot in the wall, where the washer and dryer was, now washing would be sort of free for us. I went into my room and changed into some grey cargo shorts with a grey tank top with blue flowers on it. I made sure the top of my breasts was visible to Shane. I came out of the bedroom and went into the living room area where Shane was waiting. He smiled as I approached him and he came in then gave me a kiss on the lips lightly.

'You look beautiful," Shane said. "Ella ready to go too?"

I put my finger up for a moment. "Ella! you ready to go to the store."

"Yes, mommy!" Ella yelled back.

In a few moments we both could see Ella booking out of her room and was still dressed in her outfit. We went out of the house and I locked the door behind me then we went and got in the van. I started it up and we drove to Walmart to pick up the necessary items we were missing for was drink, fresh fruits and some snacks. He also found a cane that he bought for himself to use without the walker, Shane paid for it all with his credit card then we loaded the back of the van with the groceries. I took him to a US bank in town and he withdrew cash from there with his check card. Ella and I stayed in the van waiting for him patiently since it only took a few moments. He got in and handed me another thousand dollars then buckled up.

"Can you take me to Vinny's gym?" Shane asked. "I want to see if he's there."

I looked up Vinny's gym on my google and the address popped up so I put it in my GPS so we could find it since I didn't know if he could remember. We drove there and I put the radio on since were not really talking to each other. Shane became really silent for some reason once we got into the parking lot of the Kenwood strip mall. On the google maps it was supposed to Vinny's Boxing and fitness Gym. The front read, Steward's 9 rounds fitness center, my heart lurched in my throat, I'm sure

Shane wasn't excited either.

"What the hell," he whispered.

I touched his arm. "You, ok?"

He shook his head no and got out of the van, luckily, we were parked or I swear he would have jumped out. Shane started walking kind of fast, using the cane to help him with his bad left foot, heading into the gym. I got Ella out and we followed behind as fast as we could, entering the fitness center. Shane was standing next to the front desk, where an elderly black man was sitting behind. He looked a lot like Morgan Freeman, with no earrings in the ears and was wearing a white summer button up short sleeve shirt, white Fedora, black slacks. Shane was trying to talk to him but he really looked upset.

"Where's Vinny?" Shane asked.

Virgil Steward stood up from his chair." Vinny sold this gym to me mister....?"

"Shane Avis," he replied.

"Avis, Shane "Lightning Fists" Avis, a pleasure to make you acquaintance," Virgil said. "I am sure under better circumstances; I am surprised that Vinny did not let you know."

"I saw him in Vegas five months ago with Darius Williams, why would he sell since he had a champion," Shane said flustered.

"That was the reason why, Mr. Avis, he went to Las Vegas with his champion to train him," Virgil replied. "I do apologize that no one informed you, I do work with some Pro fighters here if you would be interested training here, it would be the same price 30 a month and a locker fee."

I looked at Shane, he almost looked like he was going to break down in tears but he caught himself and tried to be cool.

"I will think about it Mr. Steward, do you know if Evan Abrams still works as a cut man around in Duluth?" Shane asked.

Steward smiled. "Indeed, he does Mr. Avis, he helps me in the corner for the Golden Gloves championship and some of my pro fighters."

Shane nodded. "All right, thank you Mr. Steward. I'm sorry if I sounded loud to you. I was really surprised since I had worked with Vinny for two years."

Virgil produced a business card from his desk and handed it to Shane. "Here, just call if you're interested and I understand Mr. Avis when you get certain surprises, have a good day."

Shane took it then turned to me and took my hand in his so I could help him out of the gym. We got into the van, Shane pulled his phone and tried to call someone, it went straight to an automated voice, saying the line had disconnected. He stopped the call, setting the phone on his leg then staring out at the gym from the van. I felt sorry for him since he just lost one of his friends. I put the van in drive and headed back to Trinity Road to our house. He didn't say anything, just put his hand on my bare leg, staring out the window. I put my right hand over his and held it gently as we headed back home. I parked in the driveway once we got there and Shane got out, getting his walker out. He put a twenty-four pack of water on it and a bag of groceries on it then went to the front door, unlocking. I handed Ella a few easy bags then took the rest and headed into the house. We set all the groceries onto the Dining room table then Shane went rolling out again with the walker. He grabbed two twenty-four packs of Diet Coke and Diet Mountain Dew from the back of the van and set it on the walker seat. I grabbed the milk and juice from the back, carrying it to the house, following Shane. We set the rest of the groceries on the dining room table then Shane put away his walker. He gave me a quick look then a kiss on my cheek.

"I'm going to ride my exercise bike for a while," Shane said.

I nodded. "In a few hours I will make some supper for us,"

He went away still looking devastated and I felt sorry for him,

I just wanted to put my arms around him with a nice hug. I put all of the groceries away in the fridge so we had some fresh fruit and drink. From a small chest freezer that was connected to the kitchen counter, I found some prime steaks, frozen mixed vegetables. I set them aside then got all the pans ready for cooking on the nice flat electric cooking stove. Ella had come out of her room so I turned on the TV to watch some kid's cartoon on Boomerang channel. I just hoped at suppertime Shane would be in a better mood when he came to eat.

Chapter Fifteen

Shane

I was really pissed off, not only did Vinny sell the gym, he got rid of his phone number and didn't even tell me he was at least leaving Minnesota. If I would have known that, I would have at least just stayed with my parents in Vegas. I would have found a trainer in Las Vegas to take me on again. I knew I shouldn't rage about it; I may have another trainer in Virgil if I could get healthy enough. I now have Courtney and Ella as my family so it was my duty to get better so I could support them. I got on the bike and just kept increasing the power to the bike so it would be harder to pedal. I must have been pedaling for at least an hour, my legs felt dead tired from pedaling so much. I stopped and began stretching my legs out, taking my time so I could get the tightness out of them I looked at my watch, it was about five in the afternoon now, just about dinnertime. It was getting easier, walking around, now I was just using a cane for some balance for the left foot. I walked out to the living room area where I could see Ella and Courtney watching some cartoon tv show on the Boomerang channel. Ella was sitting on the floor close to the tv, while Courtney sat on the couch. I went and sat down next to Courtney and put my arm around her shoulders. She gave me a smile and I gave her a quick kiss on the lips, then I tuned into the cartoon they were watching, Jonny Quest.

"God, that was my favorite cartoon growing up," I said.

"You feeling any better?" Courtney asked.

"Yes, I am Courtney," I said. "I saw you and it made my day better again."

Courtney leaned into me, putting her head on my shoulder while we watched the cartoons in silence for a while then a buzzer went off. She untangled herself from me then went in the kitchen and pulled out a big baking dish that looked like it had Tater Tot hot dish. Courtney put it in the middle of the table then started to go get plates. I pushed myself up from the couch then went into the kitchen to help grab plates to set the table. I set it all up and Courtney dished up all of our plates. Ella got herself away from the tv and came into the dining room to sit at the table with us. Courtney said a prayer that surprised me.

"God, thank you for this family and all the happiness that you have given me," Courtney said.

We all said. "Amen."

Looking at my beautiful Angel, just made me want to kiss her, even in front of Ella, which I did since I could hear Ella giggle. I pulled back with a smile and finally let go of her hand.

"I probably should call my father tonight to let him know the bad news," I said.

"Yeah, that would be a good idea," Courtney said. "Are you going to take Virgil up on his offer to train at his gym?"

"I think so but I might ask my father if he knows anything about this guy since he did live here in town while he was growing up," I said. "Plus, he did some real estate here for a while in Duluth until he moved to Florida when I graduated from high school and joined the Navy."

"I'm guessing he made better money there?" Courtney asked.

"Yeah, it was when I joined the navy, he decided to leave," I said.

The hot dish turned out to be Shepherd's pie with the instant mashed potatoes that was in the cabinets. I realized we forgot to get some potatoes or tater tots when we had gone shopping today. Courtney had made some instant gravy that she had found which I poured some on to my food. Ella copied me and put some gravy on hers then we began digging into the food, it tasted really good for something whipped up in an hour. I was still really screwed up that Vinny would just not ell me where he was going but I guess we were not that good of friends to let me know. I was figuring on getting up real early for a run with my walker every day for about two weeks then go get myself hooked up with Virgil. I think I would make sure I would take Ella and Courtney for walks with me also. The more I did for my legs the better I would be walking and would be able to train again. I really wanted to make love to Courtney since now I knew she had feelings for me too. I needed to get rid of my chivalry or was I holding back since I would feel I betrayed Christine and Tristan? I think maybe the confusion of that part was messing me up and holding me back from giving my self totally to Ella and Courtney.

"Tomorrow, would you like to go check out Enger Tower?" I asked.

"Yes, I would love to check it out," Courtney said. "I'm sure Ella would like it as well."

"Okay, sounds good," I said. "I can kind of use that as my training then. Well, anything walking wise helps."

"Yeah, no problem, Shane," Courtney said. "That's what I'm here for."

All of the plates I had were all black which were not the ones I had with Christine; I'm thinking my father switched out the plates. I must say everything was accounted for; I just hope he got my snow blower stored in the shed. We finished eating and I picked up the dirty dishes from everyone then went in the kitchen. I washed up all the dirty dishes we made then took out some containers from the cabinets. I put the rest of the Shepherd's pie into the containers and washed up the baking dish. Courtney set the containers in the refrigerator while I put the dishes away in the cupboards. I went into my room and started to rummage in the closet to find another boardgame that we could play. It was The Dungeon boardgame that TSR used to have that was basically an easy Dungeons and Dragons game. I brought it out to the dining room table then set it up for us. I had the game with my brother Trey when we were growing up so it gave me good memories of the time we had together. I showed Courtney and Ella how the game was played before starting. We must have played for over an hour until we all started dying from trying to get the real big treasure. Ella beat both Courtney and I with the most treasure made so I put the game back in the box.

"So how did you like that, Ella?" I asked.

"It was fun, Papa," Ella said.

I smiled. "I'm glad Ella, you did really well in the game. I will go put this away and we can watch a movie."

I brought the game and stuffed it on a shelf in the closet then went to the living room to snuggle up to Courtney on the couch. Ella sat on the couch beside Courtney in front with her arm around her waist. They were watching the Incredibles two, it was really funny so I enjoyed watching the movie with them. After the movie, I decided I would stretch more then ride the exercise bike for a while.

"I'm going to workout for a bit," I said, giving Courtney a brief kiss on the cheek.

I untangled myself then headed to my bedroom and began stretching my legs before getting on the exercise bike to use. I listened to some music on my iPod as I pushed myself hard, making the tension tougher on my legs. I did this until they could barely move then got off and began stretching again. I also worked on pushups and sit-ups until I was completely tired, just lying on the floor on my back. I looked at my watch; it read nine PM; it was time for me to take all of my meds before bed. I heard a knock on my door and Courtney walked in, with her grey gym shorts and grey V-neck t-shirt, with no glasses on. She held out her hand and I took it to help me off the floor. I almost landed into her arms as I got up off the floor, I could smell the Lavender on her skin as it aroused my senses. I could tell Courtney wasn't wearing a bra underneath the t-shirt as I could see they hung a little bit lower; nipples erect in the t-shirt. I began kissing her, my hands were exploring all of her body. I pulled her to my bed and we continued touching each other through our clothes. I was about to go underneath the t-shirt when I heard Ella's voice calling out.

"Mommy! Can I get a drink please?" Ella asked.

I could tell she was getting closer so I stopped and touched Courtney's face before we broke away from each other. Ella came into view while I dried the sweat off my face with a towel, I was finally standing up. Courtney went to Ella, taking her hand and guiding her to the kitchen where the refrigerator awaited. I grabbed a t-shirt and sleep pants then headed to the bathroom so I could take a cold shower. I finished and got dressed, getting out of the bathroom to say goodnight to Ella. I could hear Courtney must have been telling her a story as I got near the bedroom. I looked in seeing Courtney reading a book, it looked like Red Riding Hood, next to Ella's bed in a chair. It brought a smile to my face, thinking about when I used to read a book or just tell a He-Man story to Tristan before he went to bed. I stood in the doorway, listening to Courtney using some different voices for the characters in the book. Even that brought a smile to my face, this was truly God letting me find another family. I waited until Courtney finished then I went into the room to give Ella kiss on the forehead.

"Goodnight, Cinderella," I said.

"Goodnight, momma and papa," Ella said.

I took Courtney by the hand and pulled her to my bedroom, shutting the door behind me. I ripped off my shirt then I helped get her t-shirt off. The light was off but I could see her heavy breasts in the dark. I helped her out of her shorts and I got out of my sleep pants so we would both be naked.

Chapter Seventeen

Courtney

Shane had pulled me into his room and surprisingly I let him since I knew where this would lead, once he shut the door behind him. I saw him rip off his t-shirt, showing his ripped body from all the training he was doing then he moved to me. I let him take off my shirt as we kissed passionately and then he pulled my shorts down. He guided me to the bed when we were both naked, using his hands in every way possible. When he entered me, it definitely was bigger then all 6 men that I had dated from the past. I felt I was in heaven, while we were going in a slow rhythm, kissing and touching. I knew that this was actual love making not just a savage quickie by my employer. While he was about to orgasm, he whispered something to me.

"My Angel," Shane whispered then shuddered.

Hearing that term made me shudder with a nice orgasm as he brushed my hair back then kissed me all over before laying back in bed. I cuddled Shane in his bed, luckily it was a full size so we could cuddle without being cramped. We lay there in silence for a time, with Shane just stroking my hair and body.

"I hope this wasn't to fast for you," Shane said. "I tried to hold off as long as I could but I am in love with you."

I kissed Shane on the lips. "As I am in love with you Shane. I never have been so happy in my life when I am with you."

I could see a smile in the darkness. "I prayed to God to be happy again and he gave me you and Ella."

He brushed my hair back from out of my face as began kissing my lips softly then felt my body with one hand. He flipped me on my back and entered me again, getting into a steady rhythm again that was leaving me breathless, as he kissed my lips. It didn't take long before I let out a groan of ecstasy as he came inside me. He lay back on his pillow then I leaned my head on his chest. I was definitely hoping that this relationship would last between us since he was a better lover than I had hoped.

I fell asleep in Shane's arms and woke up in the morning, hearing Shane grunting while doing pushups. From all the exercise, Shane definitely was getting his muscle tone back. I got up and put my shirt on with shorts so I could go to the bathroom since I knew Ella would be awake soon. I got that over with and started making some Eggs and bacon in the kitchen. Ella came out in her PJs and turned on the tv, putting it on the Boomerang channel. I set the table with plates and put the silverware down then put the food on the plates with a piece of toast. I went to get Shane to let him know breakfast was ready, he was just coming out of his bedroom.

"Oh, I was just coming to tell you breakfast was ready," I said.

He smiled. "I know I could smell it; it made my belly start growling so I was coming to the kitchen."

He took my hand and pulled me back to the kitchen so we could all sit down to start eating the breakfast. It was a good breakfast and Shane made sure he did all the dishes, pans after we finished eating everything. This definitely was my kind of guy I wanted who shared in everyday activities with his partner. After that, Shane went into his room and got a thick DVD, that read He-Man and the Masters of the Universe.

"Ella lets watch some He-man and She-Ra," Shane said.

He put the DVD in the player and I could hear the 80's version come on while I went to change into different clothes. I put on another V-neck blue t-shirt with blue cargo shorts, I had cleaned up a bit with some bath wipes before putting the clothes on. I pulled my hair back into a pony tail then put my glasses back on. I went out there, the clock on the wall read it was after ten AM so I went over to Shane and Ella.

“Are we still going to Enger Tower?” I asked.

Shane looked over at me and smiled. “Yes, we are. I will go get dressed Courtney.”

He tickled Ella before he wandered back to his bedroom then I told Ella to go changed so we could go to the Tower. It took only about ten minutes for both Shane and Ella to get out of their rooms, dressed, ready to go. Shane was wearing blue jeans, Mount Rushmore t-shirt, with sketcher tennis shoes and Ella was wearing her favorite She-Ra shirt, blue jean shorts. I got my purse that had everything I needed for the drive to Enger Tower. I got into the van and started it up, while Shane got Ella into her booster seat, buckling her in. He then jumped into the passenger side while I put the GPS on to get to the Tower. It took us thirty minutes to get there with parking looking we would have to park a distance from the Tower. We got out of the van and all began to walk to get up to the Tower. Once we got there, I could tell this was not going to be fun getting to the top of the Tower. I was huffing and puffing by the time we got to the top to check out the scenery. Shane grabbed me by the waist to keep me close as we looked out of the Tower seeing the city from afar. Shane picked up Ella like a paper weight so she could see, just keeping her close to the opening so she could look out.

“What do you think Ella?” Shane asked

“It’s pretty cool papa,” Ella said.

We then got a picture done by some couple we ran into at the top before we decided to go down the stairs of the Tower. I found a short trail to some Chinese gong or Japanese garden that was part of the park near the Tower. We checked it out, with Shane helping Ella to use the gong so she could hear it. We went another trail, ending up under a canopy of some sort but we could see the Lake and the park pointe bridge with a boat going under the bridge. Ella pointed then Oohed and Ahhed as it went under the bridge. I was glad it was sunny out today so we could do this for Ella. We got some Ice cream from a food truck that was parked in the parking lot.

“So how did you like it guys?” Shane asked.

“I thought I was going to pass out before making it to the top,” I chuckled.

“It was really cool, Papa!” Ella said.

I knew at some point I would have to tell Shane I could not have anymore kids since I had to have an operation for some cancer that would have killed me. It was taken out of my reproduction area of my body so now I could not produce anymore kids since they had to tie my tubes. I could tell he was a very caring man so I didn’t think it would be a problem with Shane if I told him.

“Tomorrow, I have to get my prosthetics from the Essentia clinic foot doctor,” Shane said. “You can drive me in the morning?”

“Sure, we can do that,” I said.

He finished his ice cream cone then we headed to the van and got in so we could head back to the house. It was probably around after noon that we got back to the house so I could make some lunch for all of us.

“Why don’t you get on your laptop and get the website you use so we can pay off your van,” Shane said.

I looked surprised but said. “Okay, Shane.”

I got my Chromebook out then switched it on then I fixed the WI-FI password into it so I could use the internet that we had. I got on the website for the car dealership I used for the loan on the vehicle to make a payment. Shane handed me his credit card, which was a Capital One gold standard card.

‘How much do you have on this?” I asked.

"I think it's a 50,000-dollar credit limit," Shane said. "I was making a lot of money in the boxing ring."

"Oh, wow that's crazy," I said then made the payment of two thousand. "I'm home free from it now, just car insurance."

"Ok, good," Shane said. "In a couple of weeks, we will get the front brakes done and change the tires ok."

I smiled at him. "Thank you, Shane."

"That reminds me, I need to make a payment on the card with my own laptop, "Shane said. "And your welcome, Courtney."

Shane got up and went into his own bedroom and brought his Apple laptop out to the dining room table. He turned it on, waiting it for to boot up while I made some some ham sandwiches with a few potato chips for us. He must have logged on to the website then using his check card through US bank he made a payment on the site. Shane then powered down his computer then came over to the dining room table to eat lunch. We talked with each other about going to the fish museum down by Amsoil arena and checking out on a Thursday after he got his prosthetic for his left foot to stay in place better. Once he finished lunch we sat and watched some tv for a while with Ella. Shane actually was cuddling me on the couch as we watched SpongeBob for a while on the Nickelodeon channel. We stayed like this for a while until Shane got restless and got up from the couch.

"I am going to go running on my machine for a while, Courtney," Shane said.

I nodded. "OK, I will let you know when I start making supper."

Shane went to his bedroom and closed the door behind him, I could hear the start of his electric treadmill began running. I worked with Ella, doing some coloring in her She-Ra coloring books for at least an hour. I then got out some steaks from the freezer, got some mac and cheese with mixed vegetables for both side dishes. I went and checked on Shane to let him know I was cooking dinner. I could see him holding on the side bars of the treadmill, doing a light jog and getting a nice sweat going.

"I will be making dinner shortly, if you're interested," I said.

He looked over and smiled. "I will always be interested; I will be there in about fifteen minutes."

I went back to the kitchen to get cooking and the side dishes only took fifteen minutes to get done while I fried up the steaks in a pan. I was finishing up on the steaks, I felt an arm around my waist and lips kissing my neck.

"You look sexy cooking," Shane said.

I turned around and gave him a kiss on the lips. "Why thank you, boss."

Ella giggled then Shane hurried to get over to his usual spot at the table near Ella then dished up the side dishes on all the plates while I finished the steaks. I put a steak on each plate while Shane got forks and knives. He cut up Ella's steak into small pieces so she would be able to eat it then we did a prayer at the table.

"Thank you, Lord, for my momma and papa," Ella said.

Both I and Shane smiled at the prayer." Alright, let's eat."

We ate in silence for a while just enjoying the food and the quiet of the night that was closing in for us. This was a very good week for this new family and I hoped it would continue.

Chapter Eighteen

Shane

I slept in the same bed as Courtney without attacking her this time and just cuddling all night with less nightmares than expected. I got up first at like seven in the morning and started my stretching exercises with pushups and sit-ups. My grunting at actually woke up Courtney and I stopped for a moment to kiss her on the lips. It brought a beautiful smile from her.

“Good morning, Beautiful,” I said.

“Good morning, my sexy hunk of a man,” Courtney replied.

She gave me an extra kiss on the lips then we both got clothes with us and went into the bathroom. We made love in the shower until we were both satisfied then got dressed for the day. Courtney went and got Ella up then helped with some clothes then had her shower so she would be clean. I entered the kitchen and grabbed a few frying pans so I could whip up scrambled eggs with bacon. I also put four pieces of toast in the toaster, once they came out, I buttered them, setting them on a plate. When I finally saw Courtney and Ella, the food was mostly set out, ready to eat.

“Wow, I thought I was cooking this time,” Courtney said.

“I like to cook also so I figured since I am getting better, I would put in my time for the family,” I said.

Courtney blushed. “Why thank you, Shane.”

“You’re welcome, Courtney,” I said.

We all hungrily ate up all the food then I did the dishes while

Courtney got Ella a few books for my clinic appointment for the Prosthetic foot brace. I got my cane and followed Courtney out to the van. I helped little Ella into her booster chair, buckling her in then gave her a kiss on the forehead.

"Ready for the ride Little She-Ra," I said.

"I'm ready papa," Ella said.

I got in and buckled up so we could get out of the driveway to get on the road to get to third street where the Essentia health clinic was. We parked in a ramp then parked as close as possible to the doors going into the clinic. I held Courtney's hand as we walked in the clinic then got on an elevator that took us to the right floor. We waited in the foot doctor's office until Doctor Glenn Epstein stepped out to greet me. I got up and shook his hand then followed him to his office while Courtney stayed with Ella. We got into the office then he pointed at a chair next to the front of his desk.

"Have a seat, Mr. Avis," he said.

I sat down and he brought out a small metal foot brace then began taking off my left shoe so he could put the brace on. It inserted into the shoe then he had to force the foot a little to get the shoe back on. He pulled a strap across the calf muscle to help keep it on then stood up, motioning me to stand up. I got up and moved around with the new brace on with out the cane, with no fear of tripping myself up. I felt that my balance was way better and I could walk a lot better with the brace on.

"Wow, this is a whole different me with the brace on," I said.

"It should keep your foot stabilized while walking and you can actually jog with it on," The doctor said. "If you decide to do that again."

I smiled. "Thanks, Doc, I will probably be jogging with the brace on so I can get training again."

I went over some paperwork for the brace and what I was doing now for working out with the foot, he added some exercises that was supposed to help make it stabile. I walked out of the office with a smile on my face as I walked toward Courtney without the cane. Ella got up and came rushing to my waist, hugging me.

"Shane, that's fantastic, you're walking without the cane," Courtney said.

"I know right," I said. "I will be able to start training in two weeks once I get used to the brace."

"Well, what do you want to go do now?" Courtney asked.

"How about we go down and take a bot ride since it's nice out," I said.

Courtney smiled. "That sounds wonderful."

We went back through the maze of hallways to get back to the elevators to go down to the floor we needed to get to the ramp. I was ecstatic with the brace on, walking all over without the cane as we walked through the ramp to get to the van. I helped Ella get in to her booster seat then got on to the passenger side, closing the door behind me. My cellphone started buzzing to life in my pocket so I pulled it out to answer.

"Hello," I said.

"Hey kiddo, it's your pops, I got some bad news for you," My father said.

"Yeah, what's up Dad?" I asked.

"I was only able to get you 200,000 out of the life insurance policy since Christine's parents sued for 300,000, even though you took care of the funeral expenses while being in the coma, trying to recover from the broken bones and blunt force trauma," Don said. "At least the judge didn't think you purposely almost killed yourself for the insurance money."

Courtney was driving to where the boats were downtown near Lake Superior while I was talking to my dad on speaker phone.

I gritted my teeth. "Why do they think it's my fault, it was the truck driver who fell asleep at the wheel's fault. I tried swerving and I went into the railing, I wish Christine's parents didn't think I did that on purpose."

"I know kiddo but at least you got half the life insurance policy since you will need it before making any kind of comeback in the ring," Don said. "Try not to let you bother you, you have enough stress trying to recover Shane."

"Yeah, that's true Dad, thanks for all the help," I said.

"I just want you to have some sort of quality of life, bud," Don said. "Alright, you keep your head up and say hi to Courtney and Ella for us."

"I will thank, pops," I said.

I smiled at Courtney. "At least he likes you and Ella."

"He sounds like it anyways," Courtney said as she parked in the Amsoil lot.

We all got out of the van and I led them down the street towards the lake, where the Vista Queen was sitting in the water. We were still next to the Amsoil arena but one side was the gift shop and ticket place for the Vista Queen. I pulled Courtney behind me, now pretty confident about my walking with the brace. I almost felt normal with it on, I stopped at the counter and got three tickets for the Vista Queen. I picked up a t-shirt for Ella and Courtney with the Vista Queen ships on front of the shirts. I also got some Stuffed Vista Queen ship that Ella loved holding on too. The time flew by as we kept looking at all the cool stuff in the gift shop before we got on board for the ride. We stood in line for a few minutes then we got on board and got a seat inside the boat near a window. I let Ella sit on my lap as we got under way, where I pointed out certain landmarks I knew from my childhood. I looked over at Courtney and surprisingly she gave me a kiss on the lips.

"Thank you, my angel," I said.

"This has been the best week so far," Courtney said.

I grabbed her hand. "It sure has, love."

We watched the scenery go by while Ella got excited pointing at a little island or even a merchant marine ship that was sailing to the docks. It was officially now 6 months since the accident and would be creeping into the seventh month in July. I believe with God's help I had finally gotten my life back on track. He gifted me another family that loved me and needed me to be there, this time there would be no mistakes. Once we got back to the dock, we got off the Vista Queen and walked over to the William A Irvin cargo ship so we could get a tour. We wandered the ship checking everything out, while Ella asked a million questions pointing at everything. It was about another good hour before we began to head home since it had been already about 3 hours and no lunch. They were both happy and seemed to have had a good time near the boats. We parked the van in the driveway and I got out right away so I could help Ella out of her booster seat. Courtney went to the mailbox and picked up the mail then headed back as I opened the front door to the house.

"You got some bills from the hospital, babe," Courtney said.

It was surprising that the words that came out of her mouth was so easy now as being a couple, not boss and worker anymore. I took the bills from her hands as we went in, kissing her cheek.

"Thanks love," I said.

I set the bills on the end of the kitchen counter while we got some food picked out to cook for supper. Which was pork chops, instant mashed potatoes and can of green beans, I started making the instant mashed potatoes while Courtney cooked the pork chops. I knew she wanted this as much as me since our time in bed. I wanted to move forward with my life but not to forget Christine and Tristan. I enjoyed that time also but this was what God wanted me to do. I opened the big family size can of green beans and put them into a sauce pan to heat up. I turned on the tv and on the news was me. They showed me coming out of the clinic with Courtney and Ella, then they showed the wreckage of Shane's car with blood around it. The male reporter, a handsome Max Drevis began speaking on tv.

"Today, we saw number one middle weight contender Shane "Lightning Fists" Avis come out of the Essentia clinic, wearing a foot brace. He looks like he finally is getting well after a major car crash in Las Vegas after his big win. Shane lost his wife and child with sustaining life-threatening broken bones to his body and head trauma. We hope out hometown hero gets his comeback soon," The reporter said.

I could feel tears roll down my face, looking at the tv. It aggravated me that someone would be that cold to put me on the news. Courtney must have turned off the green beans so they wouldn't burn then I could feel her arm around my waist.

Chapter Twenty

Courtney

We were cooking and getting the table set up, when the tv news had come on with us coming out of the clinic. They also showed the horrible accident that Shane survived from in full color, God really saved him since the car was totally destroyed, with blood on the rocks. I could see Shane having tears roll down his eyes as he looked at this and I went over to comfort him. I put my arm around his waist and turned off the stove so his side of the food would not burn. He wiped away the tears then turned to me and kissed me on the lips gently. Shane then went back to setting the food on the table as I finished up on cooking the pork chops in the frying pan. I put the pork chops on a plate and set it next to the side dishes we made so we could dish up our pates. Ella grabbed our hands for prayer.

"Thank you, God, for my papa, that he didn't leave this earth after the crash," Ella said.

Shane smiled. "Amen, Ella."

He got up from his chair and kissed Ella's forehead then went and sat back in his chair to finally dig into his food. I smiled at the gesture, Shane made, he really looked happy to be here with both Ella and I. Once we finished eating, Shane was cleaning up the dishes while I got something on tv for Ella to watch. I was surprised since he never would let me do them and would let take care of Ella before I helped him. I put the dishes away and Shane then went and began talking with Ella while they watched a Disney show on tv. I thought to myself, Christine had been lucky woman to have Shane when she was alive if he was like this all the time. I went to the couch where Shane sat and cuddled him a bit as we watched tv together for a while. After the show, Shane broke away and gave me a kiss.

"I'm going to workout for a while hon," Shane said.

"Alright," I said.

Shane left me then I picked a reality kid baking competition on the cooking channel for me and Ella to watch. It was about Nine at night by the time Shane was done working out and I put Ella to bed. I was naked and getting ready to put my pajamas when Shane had entered the room, closing the door behind him. He was just wearing sleeping shorts and could see he was excited as he guided me to the bed to make love to me. We did this until we were both satisfied and tired then we lay in the bed with my head on his chest. He was stroking my back and my buttocks as we lay in the darkness, just cuddling in bed.

"I think tomorrow I want to get set up with Virgil, to start to get ready to box again," Shane said.

"I think that would be a good idea, you seem to be getting better and you should use a good trainer to help you get back to your old self," I said.

"I just don't understand why Vinny left without telling me," Shane said. "That really bothers me."

"I understand but you should take Virgil up on his offer and move forward," I said.

"Your right," Shane said. "We can go there after lunch tomorrow to set everything up."

I kissed his chest then we began to make love again until we both orgasmed and fell asleep this time after the lovemaking. The morning was the same, Shane was in the other room working out while I dressed in my pajamas. I went and got Ella up so she could take a shower for the day and dress. I went and made

French toast for the family while Shane showered and dressed himself quickly. Shane was wearing a V-neck t-shirt, jeans, and tennis shoes, his chest was now getting more formed from all the working out and the muscle tone to his arms. He came to the table kissing me on the lips then Ella's forehead as he sat down at the table. He must have been wearing the brace since he was walking without his cane for support and he almost looked normal. He looked at the French toast surprised.

"Wow, this looks good, I love French toast," Shane said.

"Thanks, it should be good," I said.

I had made sure there was butter out and syrup out on the table so we could add it to the French toast. We ate in silence for a while as Shane looked at his medical bills and was just shaking his head.

"I really hope my medical insurance kicks in and starts paying, I owe 350,000 dollars to that hospital," Shane said.

"In a month, they will send you another bill and hopefully your insurance will be on that one," I said.

"I hope so, I hate having to call to see if anything is working since you get stuck on the phone for an hour just trying to get someone," Shane said.

He put the bills aside then dressed his French toast and began eating with us, looking not as stressed as he was looking at the bills. He looked over at me and smiled.

"I have an idea for dinner," Shane said.

"What's that?" I asked.

"We pick up tater tots, cream of mushroom soup, green beans, hamburger, cheese for tater tot hot dish," Shane said.

"Yeah, that sounds really good, Shane," I said.

He finished his French toast then went over to the kitchen sink and washed his dishes up while we finished eating. I did the rest of the dishes while Shane got the mail and separated the mail up between us. I had a few letters from my sister and folks from Iowa, Shane had a card then some more bills from the hospital. He set it on the dining room table then he grabbed the kitchen trash and brought it out to the dumpster we have next to the building. I replaced the trash bag then followed Shane outside with Ella, locking the front door. I drove Shane over to the gym, Virgil owned and parked in the Lot. Down a way from the gym, was a Grocery store in the strip mall so we could shop after Shane got set up. Shane walked into the boxing gym while we stayed outside. I could see Shane and Virgil talking while Shane filled out some paperwork and he handed cash to Virgil. Shane smiled then shook Virgil's hand then came out of the gym to greet us.

“How did it go?” I asked.

“It went well, I need to be here by ten AM then I have to work out for two hours at least,” Shane said.

“Well, it's the beginning of trying to get your career back at least,” I said.

He took my hand. “Yes, it is.”

Shane pulled me towards the grocery store and Ella, holding a hand each, we stepped in and got a shopping cart. Shane pushed the cart to help his balance a little while I had Ella and we picked up all the ingredients to make tater tot hot dish. We paid for all the stuff then we headed back to the van. Shane got Ella in then jumped into the passenger side of the van.

“Let's stop at the Discount tire shop and get this van some new tires,” Shane said.

“Are you sure?” I asked.

“Yeah, you should be ready for winter,” Shane said. “I don't trust myself driving just yet.”

“Ok, let's do it,” I said.

We got to the tire shop at the Central entrance location and waited in the lobby while they put some brand-new tires on the van. Shane showed me and Ella on his phone about a taconite mine museum going north up to the Iron Range in Chisolm, Minnesota.

"Would you like to see that, Ella? "Shane asked.

"Yeah, it would be fun papa," Ella said.

"If it's nice on the weekend, we can head up North to check it out," Shane said.

A guy in a Discount tire shirt waved us over to the lobby counter and we headed over to him.

"The tires are all installed and your ready to go," he said. "The price is 350 dollars for everything."

Shane took out his credit card and paid for the tires while I preoccupied Ella in watching some tires get put on a Toyota. He finished with the paperwork then handed it to me so we could go to the van that they parked by the front door. Shane helped Ella back into her booster seat then buckled her in then he got into his passenger spot. We headed back to the house and the ride seemed to be a lot smoother with the new tires. I parked in the driveway close to the ramp to the house. We got out and Shane went to the mailbox to check the mail while I got Ella out of the van. Shane caught up to me, placing his hand on my waist as we went into the house, it brought a smile to my face. He put the mail on the coffee table this time then helped get a big baking dish from a top cabinet.

He placed it on the kitchen counter then got the ground beef out and started cooking it. I opened all the cans and placed them near the stove so once he was done, he could get them easily. He finished seasoning and grounding up the beef then mixed it with the vegetables a can of mushroom soup. He put it all in the baking dish then added the tater tots to the top layer with cheese. I put it in the oven after I was done setting the table then Shane went to change in his relaxing clothes for the night. Shane went to workout while Ella and I watched another show together. We must have watched 2 shows since it was already nine PM again, time flew. I helped Ella get ready for bed then I read her the little red riding hood for her bedtime story.

Chapter Twenty-one

Shane

I had done some stretching then jogged on the running machine for 30 minutes then did my pushups and sit-ups. I have a mirror in my room so I shadow boxed for another 20 minutes until I was nice and sweaty then showered. I put some other pajamas I had then walked to Ella's room since I knew she would be getting ready for bed, to kiss her goodnight. I heard Courtney's voice as she told the story of little red riding hood. I waited until she was finished then walked in as Courtney gave her a kiss goodnight, I kissed her as well.

"Goodnight, Cinderella," I said.

"Night, momma and papa," Ella said.

I took Courtney's hand and pulled her to her bedroom then closed the door behind me as began kissing the woman passionately. We made love for an hour until we were both satisfied then she lay her head on my chest, cuddling. I looked over at the clock and it read about eleven at night. Courtney spoke and what came out surprised me.

"Just to let you know, I can't have children anymore since I had to tie my tubes," Courtney said.

"That's alright Courtney, I really just want you but you just had a valuable package with you," I said.

She looked up at me then I kissed her on the lips gently. "I love you, Shane."

"I love you my Angel," I said back.

We lay in the bed in the darkness for awhile then I passed out with her on my chest, I dreamed of our vacation together. Courtney must have set an alarm since I knew today, I was supposed to workout with Virgil today. It officially had been now seven months since the accident, I hoped I was ready to start training hard again. I knew it would be 3 more months before I could get the doctor to clear me for fighting. I woke up and slapped Courtney's butt lightly then kissed her on the cheek as I got up. I put my clothes on from the night before then went to my room to change and get my duffel bag ready. I'm sure Courtney got ready and Ella for breakfast so I changed into jeans a white tank top and tennis shoes. I stuffed my bag with my boxing shorts, hand wraps, and gloves I used for training. I went out to the dining room where I could see Courtney already set out breakfast. She had made Eggs, toast and bacon all set out with the ketchup bottle sitting on the table. Ella waved at me as I sat down.

"Good morning, little She-Ra," I said and leaned over to kiss Courtney. "This looks delicious, hon."

I salted and peppered the food then put some ketchup on the scrambled eggs she made so I could have a little extra flavor. It was all good food so I must of ate pretty fast since I beat everyone eating. I took my dishes and cleaned up the pans right away so Courtney didn't have to worry about them. Once they finished, I did their dishes up and put them in the dish rack for drying along with the silverware.

"It's almost time to take you to the gym, babe," Courtney said.

"Ok, what will you be doing for over an hour before picking me up," I asked.

"I need to check the school that Ella has to go to for the application then I will do a little grocery shopping for some ingredients to make a roast," Courtney said.

"Wow, your right, August is in a week, ok let me know how it goes," I said.

I grabbed my duffel bag and Ella's hand as we walked to the van so I could get her in to her booster seat again. Once that was done, I got into the passenger seat with my duffel, buckling in then catching the time on the stereo clock, 9:15 AM. She got me there way before ten so I gave a quick kiss on the lips then I got out. I waved to Ella before I headed in the direction of the front door of the gym. I opened the door and walked in; it was pretty quiet with not a lot of people in the big gym. It had the boxing ring, 5 heavy bags, 4 speed bags, jump ropes hanging off a wall. There was a huge mirror with a rack of dumbbells, 4 weight benches, weights racked near them. He had at least ten treadmills divided up nice so you had some distance from people, which I liked.

I could see Virgil behind the front counter reading the newspaper, he looked so eerily like Morgan Freeman, it made me just shake my head. He wore his little fedora hat, Khakis, short sleeved grey button-down shirt, while he was kicked back reading. I came to the front counter then cleared my throat so he would know I was there. He closed the paper than smiled when he saw me.

"Right on time, Mr. Avis, I like punctuality in a person," Virgil said. "Are first goal, is to look at your weight today then run through some exercises."

I nodded. "That sounds fine. I haven't looked at my weight since the hospital and I was at 117 pounds."

"Ok head to the back where the locker rooms are and change into your boxing trunks then meet me near the weight room area," Virgil said.

I headed to the back which ended near the men and women's locker room, where there were showers, bathrooms for people. I went into the guy's locker room and changed out of my street clothes into my boxing workout clothes. I stuffed my bag into the locker then used my lock, that I could remember the combination too. I went to the weight room area, where Virgil was waiting for me, standing next to a scale.

“Alright, Me. Avis, please stand on the weight scale for me please,” he said.

I stepped on the weight scale and my mouth about dropped open, I only weighed 125 pounds since getting out of the hospital. Virgil didn’t look surprised and barely showed emotion when I stepped off the weight scale.

“Well, we have some work to do Mr. Avis, even to get to lightweight status for fighting again,” Virgil said. “We start the weight training to gain more muscle back then work on your balance, then start to get your Lightning fists back into shape.”

I nodded. “I expected I would have at least three more months before fighting again.”

“Mr. Avis, I think it might take about four more months to get back in the ring,” Virgil said. “I have a contact in the lower pro circuit so we can do the casinos and the St. Paul armory for fights to get your name back out there.”

“Alright, are you going to be my manager also, plus training?” I asked.

“Yes, I do that Mr. Avis and I did get a hold of Evan Abrams and he would love to be the cut man for you, for the same fee you paid him,” Virgil said.

I nodded. “My question is willing the fights be low paying like last time, about over ten thousand a fight?”

Virgil nodded his head. “The bigger fights are in the Armory; I take my cut and so will Evan so you will average three thousand a fight or a little more till you hit the big circuit. Let’s get to work Mr. Avis.”

Today was Monday so he had me do chest work, shoulders then he figured the next day would be leg day, Wednesday would be arms. My arms, chest and shoulders were sore from the workout, we only did an hour. When I got done, I changed into my street clothes and texted Courtney I was finished with the workout. I went back to the front counter, where Virgil was sitting and I took out my credit card to pay for the services of the gym for six months in advance. I handed the card to Virgil.

"Give me six months' worth Virgil," I said.

"Very good Mr. Avis, with what I saw today, four months you will be ready to fight again," he said.

He ran the card through his credit card machine then gave me a slip to sign then handed me one. I took it and stuffed it in my right front jean pocket then shook Virgil's hand.

"I will see you tomorrow at the same time tomorrow?" I spoke.

"We will see you again Mr. Avis," Virgil said.

I walked out the front door and waited for Courtney to pull up as I waited at the front of the gym entrance outside. She pulled up next to me and stopped, I got into the passenger side, giving Courtney a quick kiss on the lips that made Ella giggle. We went back home and played a boardgame with Ella, Candyland to kill some time before supper. Also, Courtney, got an application for the Lowell Elementary school so she was filling that out. Time really had flown by already to be going into August already. For supper, we had put couple of frozen pizzas into the oven for food to eat. Once that was done, Courtney cut the pizza up and divided it among us on plates. I turned the tv on so we could sit on the couch by the coffee table and have pizza while watching tv. I picked Hero 6 for a movie to watch so it would last until about nine at night, I cuddled Courtney as we watched it, Ella leaned on Courtney. When the movie ended, I helped Ella to her room and told her a bedtime story before tucking her in. This time when I went into Courtney's room, we just fell asleep holding each other instead of messing around.

The next two days were tough with more weight lifting, we

worked the legs and then the arms the next. The arm day consisted of dumbbell training and curl bar with hitting the heavy bag and doing the speed bag. In the early morning, I ran for about two miles everyday with stretching my legs and the ankles so I could get a little balance with the foot drop problem. The ankle brace helped immensely but I didn't know if I could wear it in the ring. The weekend was here and we decided to drive up to Chisolm, Minnesota for the Iron Range Museum. Courtney put it in the GPS on the cellphone and it took us a little over two hours to get there. We had fun on the trolley, listening to the guide on the trip. Inside for Ella, was a few cool games that she could do while Courtney and I checked out the site of the taconite mine. It was a few hours before we headed out then just stopped at a fast-food joint for supper, McDonalds before getting to home.

Chapter Twenty-two

Courtney

I pulled in the driveway, after having a wonderful time with Shane and Ella up on the range, learning about mines. We did our usual ritual of Shane helping Ella get out of the booster seat, unbuckling her and getting her out of the van. I went to the mailbox and grabbed the mail, while I heard the van door shut. Shane unlocked the house then we went in together, I placed the mail on the dining room table. It was mostly bills from the hospital again and a few more letters from my parents and sister. I read the letters from sister and parents, they both asked if I was going to marry Shane. It made me blush even thinking about it but it was still too soon to do that. I knew Shane had to keep training so he could get back in the ring again, fighting was in his blood and wasn't going to go away anytime soon. Shane looked at his bills not looking too happy, he looked over at me.

"Well, it's finally down to ten thousand for the bill, so I guess my insurance took care of some of the mess," Shane said.

"Well, that might not be the final bill for it so just wait until next month," I said.

Shane nodded. "Your right, I'm going to workout for a while before watching tv alright."

"Ok, see you in a while," I said.

He was gone for a while so me and Ella started playing some UNO to kill time, she won the first hand then I won the second. By that time, Shane came into the rom with some shorts and a tank top, his legs not looking as skinny as they used to be. His upper body was ripped and getting more muscle too from all the working out, he made me excited just by looking at him. It didn't help but he was also a handsome man that was funny and smart. He sat down at the dining room table with us.

"OK, deal me in Courtney," Shane said.

I dealt all seven cards after shuffling then Shane drew the card to start the game, I set the shuffled deck next to the color he drawn. I think with three people it took longer to get a winner but all of us had fun, Shane had one win. This time Shane shuffled the deck and got the game set up for another hand. The next hand, Ella won again so we stopped then watched Toy Story together at the couch. I leaned my head on his shoulder and he played with my hair for awhile just laughing at some of the funny parts of Toy Story. This definitely was new for me, that he had so much affection for me, Travis never was. I was soaking it up though, enjoying the time I was having with our new little family. Once nine pm rolled around, I put the game away while Shane put Ella to bed and read her bedtime story. I went to the bedroom to see Shane sitting in a chair, reading Cat in a hat by Doctor Suess. It made me smile as he attempted to make different voices for the characters in the book. Once Shane finished, he put the book aside then gave Ella a kiss on the forehead goodnight. He turned out the light then came to me and grabbed my hand to pull me towards my or our bedroom now. We got in and he basically ripped his clothes off then mine and we made passionate love. We went until we were both spent and tired, falling asleep.

The next day, I woke up alone by seven thirty AM and could tell Shane was working out in his old room. I took a quick shower and shaved my legs while I was at it then jumped out then brushed my hair. I rinsed my mouth out with some antiseptic mouthwash then headed to Ella's room to wake her up. I got Ella up while she went to brush her teeth, wash her face, comb her hair, I started breakfast. I made eggs in a basket with bacon, two pieces for me and Shane, one for Ella. Ella got to the table dressed in her favorite t-shirt, jean shorts and tennis shoes, she sat down and I brought her a glass of juice. Shane came after, dressed in his street clothes, Tank top, jeans, tennis shoes with duffle bag in hand. He dropped it off by the front door then came over by me to kiss my cheek, sitting down at the table.

"This looks delicious Courtney, "Shane said. "Morning, Ella.

"Morning papa," Ella replied.

"Thank you, Shane," I said with a smile.

We dug in to the food and it had turned out really good with a piece of toast to dip in the yoke of the egg. Once we finished, Shane took everyone's dirty dishes and started washing up, while I got a book for Ella to read for later. Shane finished up cleaning the dishes, pans and began wiping counter down with the dining room table. It was a little after nine am when we headed to the van and began driving toward the boxing gym. It was nice out so I figured while Shane trained, I would take Ella to a park to play. We got there after nine thirty, I stopped next to the front, he gave me a quick kiss on the lips then got out. Shane opened the side door to the van then grabbed his duffel bag then quickly kissed Ella's forehead. Shane shut the door then went into the boxing gym.

"We're going to a park Ella," I said. "Let's go have some fun while Shane works out."

I stuck in the GPS to get to the PLayfront park near the Great Lakes Aquarium near Lake Superior and Downtown Duluth. Once we got there, we parked nearby and I had to pay a parking meter for some time. It was a warm breezy day, at seventy-five degrees so at least Ella wouldn't overheat from playing in the park. I sat at a bench and kept checking my phone in case was Shane was done early. It was an hour, when Shane texted me and said he was done and taking a shower. I signaled to Ella to come over and she did.

"We need to get go get Shane from the gym, Ella," I said.

"Ok, momma," Ella said.

We got back to the van then I got Ella into her seat, she buckled herself in then I got in on the driver side to start the van up. It took us a half hour to get to the strip mall where the gym was but Shane was standing patiently outside. I smiled at him as I stopped next to him, I opened the passenger window.

"Hey handsome, going my way," I said.

Shane smiled then opened the passenger door to get in, he dropped his duffle bag at his feet this time in the front.

"Definitely, with a gorgeous woman like you," Shane replied.

We got under way, driving back towards home with both windows down so we could get some sort of breeze while driving.

"Stop at the bank before we go home there, dear," Shane said. "After that lets head to the lake walk."

"Ok," I replied.

We had stopped at Shane's bank and he went in for at least ten minutes since it was busy then came back to the van. He handed me another two thousand in cash, once he got into the van.

"Here's your money that is owed, hon," Shane said.

"OK, thank you," I said.

I put the money in my purse before we began driving to the lake walk area of Duluth, we parked in a parking lot near a hotel that was next to the lake walk. Shane got out on his side to get Ella out of the van while I got out my side. Once we locked the van, we headed to the lake walk. It was a decent day, only about seventy degrees so not to hot for walking as we strolled down the lake walk as Ella pointed at seagulls near the rocky beach. Shane took Ella to a part on the beach that was kind of flat then found a few flat stones. He showed her how to throw the stone to get it to skip across the water. When they were done with that, we went farther to the ariel bridge, near it was an ice cream shoppe. Shane bought us all cones and we got closer to the ariel bridge so we could see a few boats pass through. Shane showed us the canal park museum also as we checked it out, with all the information about ships. Inside the museum, Shane held my right hand as we explored the museum.

"So, what do you think?" Shane asked me.

"This is not bad, it's been fun and of course Ella loves it," I said.

"Well, my grandfather brought me and my brother down here as a kid and I enjoyed it so much, I joined the Navy," Shane said.

I looked at him surprisingly. "Oh, I didn't know you had a brother. Is he still around?"

Shane shook his head. "He committed suicide three years ago. He went into a great depression after his wife left him."

I squeezed his hand. "I'm sorry Shane. I am really glad I met you this last year, even if it wasn't in the best of circumstances."

I leaned towards and kissed Shane on the lips, he definitely was now my rock and he treated me with such affection and respect, way better than Travis had. We finished touring the whole museum and walked back to the van. Ella looked like she had the time of her life just doing basically the free stuff with us. Shane got her into the booster seat quickly, buckling her in so he could get into the passenger side of the van. I had already started the van up so once he got in, we could take off for home. It was a lively drive home, when Shane began a naming game with a letter for Ella. When we got home, this time Shane went and got the mail and I got Ella out of her booster seat. We went in to the house and I looked to see that I got more letters from my sister, luckily no bills. Shane dropped his duffel bag into the room then took the dirty laundry and put into the laundry machine.

I got a couple of supreme pizzas out of the freezer then got some fresh vegetables out of the fridge. I cut up some green pepper then got a can of mushrooms out and black olives, putting it on the pizza. It already had pepperoni and sausage, I just wanted to make it a little healthier. I cut some broccoli up small and put that on the pizza as well. I set the cooking level for the pizza and timer then put both pizzas into the stove then I set the table with some paper plates. Shane had busied himself getting some of my dirty clothes and Ella's to wash so the load would be bigger. Ella had turned on the tv and was watching some cartoon on the Disney channel. I sat down at the table and read my sister's letter, she was asking when she could meet Shane and wondered when we would get married. It made me blush just thinking about it since I knew this could really work as a married couple, I just didn't want to force that on Shane. He came to the table, giving me another quick kiss to the lips before sitting down.

"Another letter from the folks?' Shane asked.

"No, this time it's from my sister, she is curious about everything of course," I said.

"She older than you? "Shane asked.

"Yes, by six years and she's married with one child," I said.

Shane nodded. "That reminds me, I have to call my parents and let them know what's happening. Let me know when dinner is ready."

He got up and gave me another kiss then headed to his workout room and closed the door behind him.

Chapter Twenty-Three

Shane

When we got home, I got busy by grabbing everyone's dirty clothes and stuck them into the washing machine. After I got that done and began talking to Courtney, I realized I hadn't called my dad or mom to let them know how things were going. I headed to the now workout room since Courtney and I both agreed we couldn't stay away from each other anyways. Also, it seemed I could sleep way better with her and had less nightmares in the night. I closed the door behind me, pulling my cellphone out, hitting my father's number on speed dial. My father answered after the fourth ring.

"Hey kiddo, how's it going? You feeling better? "Don asked.

"Actually, going way better, I can now jog with a brace, plus the foot seems to be getting more stable from training," I said. "I never was able to get a hold of Vinny, he sold his gym to a Virgil Steward so now I am training with him."

"That's great, I actually knew Virgil in high school, we both played on the basketball team for Duluth Central. He did almost all the sports except hockey of course so I am not surprised, he was not a boxer at one point," Don said. "I think it's a shit thing that Vinny left you high and dry."

"Well, once I get to boxing again just to let you and mom know, I am going to ask Courtney to marry me," I said. "It will be another five months before that happens but I figured that I would let you know now so you're not surprised."

"I think you should try and live your life to the fullest their kid and she seems like a good woman anyways. I will let your mom know," Don said.

I heard a knock on the door then Courtney's voice. "Dinner's ready Shane. Just to let you know."

"Ok. Hey dad, got to let you go but will call you in a few weeks, alright, "I said.

"Alright, take care Shane, thanks for the call," Don said.

I hit the end button then got out of the workout room and headed to the dining room, where Courtney was already sitting with Ella. The pizza sat in the middle of the table with my plate next to Courtney's with a couple of pieces of pizza on it. I sat down then we held hands while Ella said a prayer.

"Dear God, thank you for this food and thank you for this family," Ella said.

We dug into the pizza and it really turned out good with the extra toppings on the pizza that Courtney added to the pizza. After we finished eating the pizzas, or most of them, I got rid of the plates then washed the pizza pans up. I then went to the couch where Ella and Courtney were sitting, snuggling up to Courtney as we watched a Disney movie. I had flipped through the channels after a while and came across The Last Starfighter on the Sci Fi channel. We watched that movie also and Ella seemed to like it so that made me happy. Our usual nine o'clock time came around and I put Ella to bed. This time, Courtney took my hand and pulled me to the bedroom. We pulled our clothes off then had mad passionate sex or love, until we were both orgasmed. We fell asleep in a cuddling position and I must have slept through the whole night as light peeked through the blinds. I got up and put some clothes on then headed to the workout room. I stretched then got on the treadmill and began jogging, doing at least two miles to get warmed up. I then did pushups and sit-ups, stretching again, after wards when Courtney came walking into the room with just a towel around her. Her brunette hair was wet and kind of curly hair, I got up and kissed her.

"I'm going to get Ella up then start making breakfast," Courtney said.

"Ok, I am going to shower now then get dressed to be ready to train," I said. "I will be out to eat in a little bit, dear."

I had in the last few days moved all of my clothes into the master bedroom with Courtney so I followed her into the bedroom to grab some clothes. I had closed the door as she was just putting a bra on but wearing no panties. I came by and gave her butt a light slap as I opened my dresser to get a white t-shirt and jogging pants, underwear, socks. I grabbed another quick kiss from Courtney then headed to the bathroom to shower. I took a fifteen-minute shower then dressed in my workout outfit for the day. I figured I would just wear the workout clothes from now on then just come home to shower and change. When I got to the dining room table, it was set up and pancakes were sitting in the middle of the table. Ella was sitting close to Courtney and there was a spot next to Ella, so I kissed Ella's forehead then sat down.

"Good morning, my little She-Ra," I said.

"Morning, Papa," Ella replied.

We dug into the pancakes and they were good since Courtney made Chocolate chip pancakes, I had slathered the butter and syrup on to make it even tastier. After I finished eating, I did up all the dishes while Ella got changed into some summer clothes. It was our normal time getting done was now after nine AM then head to the gym to drop me off. This time, I only brought a small duffel bag with me that held a towel and shower gel. I wore a fanny pack that held my wallet and house key so I didn't have to stick it into a locker at the gym. Courtney dropped me off at the gym and I headed in, waiting to see what new exercise I would do. Virgil was standing behind the counter when I came into the front entrance.

"Mr. Avis, glad you could make it, I have a few new exercises for the legs today," Virgil said. "Drop off your stuff into the locker room and let's get to work."

I headed to the back and just stuck my bag in the locker then went back out to the gym, where Virgil waited was in the free weight area. He was standing next to the Squat rack and putting weight onto the barbell.

"Go ahead and do some stretching Mr. Avis, you'll need it," he said.

I got on the floor mat and stretched out the best I could, loosening up the left calf muscle that always bunched up. Virgil had put two 35 plates on the barbell that maybe equaled about a hundred pounds onto the bar.

"I want to see where your leg strength is, if it's too much, just do what you can," Virgil said.

"Ok, I will see what I can do," I said.

I got underneath the bar and laid it on my shoulders then lifted it up to go down, which I did real slow like. It was a good thing too, I struggled to get it back up but I did it then another for good measure. Virgil helped me make sure it was racked up before I got out from under the barbell.

"Ok, looks alright Mr. Avis, lets head to leg machines I have," Virgil said.

Virgil brought me over to the weight machines he had and we began to work all the leg machine exercises on light weight. After doing that over a half hour, Virgil had me do like a crouch and like a duck walk. He helped me some but I did it mostly myself, forcing my left gimp foot to work harder than it has ever been. Virgil also had me sit on a bench then use my legs to push off the bench, doing a lot of reps on my legs. I finished off with stretching then headed to the locker room to shower off the sweat. I got back out and headed over to the counter, by the time

I was getting ready to leave people were coming into workout. Virgil smiled as he saw me.

"Good workout, Mr. Avis," Virgil said. "Tomorrow, we work on some arms with the heavy bag, speed bag, focus mitts. Try to keep the fun in bed to the weekends, Mr. Avis."

"Sounds good, coach," I said. "See you tomorrow."

I made sure I told Courtney the bad news from the coach, she took it pretty good and understood so we could wait for the weekend. We did our normal routine for the afternoon but went to Walmart to pick up ingredients to make a pot roast dinner. I also picked up a few coloring books for me and Ella so we could color together. I had picked up a few Superhero books to color, Avengers and Power puff girls. After watching few shows and eating we colored together and I picked her brain about what other stuff she liked to do.

"So do you like the old She-Ra and He-Man?" I asked Ella.

"I sure do papa," Ella replied.

"That's good to know, Ella," I said.

Courtney had joined us and helped color a few more pages before we called it quits and put Ella to bed. I fell asleep quickly with Courtney in my arms and the next day came just as quick, with the daylight poking through the curtains. I slid out from under Courtney and went to the workout room to stretch then get on the exercise bike for a few miles. Once I got done, I headed to the room to grab some clothes, I could hear Courtney talking to Ella in the kitchen. I got dressed in my workout clothes, jogging pants, and t-shirt with the fanny pack again. I knew from all the work; the left foot was getting more stable but I kept the brace on for now. We ate waffles and bacon for breakfast then I cleaned up after for everyone. Courtney dropped me off at the gym and I headed in again for more training. Virgil had me hit the heavy bag then work on the speed bag for a while. After I was done with the speed bag, Virgil signaled me to come to the boxing ring. I went over and got into the ring with him there and inside he tied a string across the ring.

"Now Mr. Avis, I want you to duck underneath and throw uppercuts, going side to side," Virgil said.

Virgil actually did a demonstration with it, going side to side, throwing the uppercuts, ducking his head in and out of the string. We did this for at least 20 minutes then we switched to the focus mitts.

"Alright, this time I want you to get connection then move your head away when I try to hit you with the focus mitt," Virgil said.

I threw fast punches to connect on the focus mitts then dodged my head from the oncoming mitt.

"Faster Mr. Avis," Virgil said.

We sped up the training with the mitts, I was barely keeping up from getting hit from the mitt but we kept this up for another thirty minutes. He stopped then brought me over to the free weight area, where we did some dumbbell training. I knew today we officially trained for two hours and would keep moving up. I was tired and my arms felt like spaghetti or whatever the old term meant. I texted Courtney and letting her know I was done working out then I hit the showers. I took a quick five-minute shower then got dressed so I could get out to wait for Courtney and Ella. I must have only stood out for ten minutes then they showed up parking next to me so I could get in. We headed home and did some fun games before we ate dinner which we just made some pizzas. The rest of the week just blurred since it was just straight up training and, on that Friday, we weighed me. Virgil stood next to weight scale he had near his office, next to the front counter.

"Alright Mr. Avis, let's see if you're moving up in weight," Virgil said.

I got on to the weight scale and I looked surprised to see it say one hundred and twenty-seven pounds with all the weight training I was doing. I definitely was getting my muscle tone back from all the weight training and exercise.

"This is a good start, Mr. Avis," Virgil said. "Just eat a little more and you will gain some more weight. I don't expect you to be at the weight I want for another month."

I stepped off the scale. "When will I be able to start sparring again?"

"Let's keep doing the stuff we have been working on for another two weeks before sparring," Virgil said. "I want you to get some speed back in the fists and get you more stable moving around the ring. That's what we will be doing on Monday."

"Alright coach," I said. "I am going to hit the showers."

I went to the locker room to shower off the sweat then dry off so I could change into some street clothes. I texted Courtney and told her I was done working out, ready to leave when she was. I walked out and headed to the front door.

"See you Monday coach," I said.

"Have a good day, Mr. Avis," Virgil said with a smile.

I waited for Courtney outside the building, drinking from my water bottle, from the duffel bag I was carrying.

Chapter Twenty-four

Courtney

I had just finished playing at Lester Park with Ella when Shane texted me, he was finished with his training. It was another kind of Lukewarm day with the sun out but I was glad it wasn't too hot out to be running around. I got Ella buckled into her booster seat and we took off to go pick up Shane from the gym. August was already flying by and Ella would be going to school soon, starting the second grade. It was a crazy realization but I was confident I would stay with Shane for the rest of my life. Everyday I couldn't wait to be waking up in his strong arms and they were now definitely strong from all the weight lifting.

I still was slightly scared if and when Shane started fighting again just because of his left foot. I could see that it was at least better, he could walk without the brace. It seemed like it wasn't dropping as much and he didn't have lift it as high. It might screw up his fighting style from before since I watched a lot of YouTube videos of his old fights. I started watching them once I was dropping him off to the gym and taking Ella to some parks. Shane was like lightning in the ring, just like the nickname proclaimed, he was always moving at lightspeed. I just hoped once he got back in the ring he would be just as fast. I picked up Shane in the front of the gym, he was wearing his Mount Rushmore shirt and jogging pants with his fanny pack. He got in and leaned over to kiss me, which always made Ella giggle.

"How was your training today?" I asked.

"It went pretty good, I'm starting to feel like my old self," Shane replied setting his bag on the floor.

"That's good to hear," I said "Any place we need to go before we head home?"

"Let's grab some hot dogs and cheddar wursts, chips, dip for grilling outside since it's nice out," Shane said. "I'm sure my old man left my gas grill in the storage shed."

We drove to Cub foods and grabbed the stuff we needed to cook out on the small deck that was connected to the ramp to the house. I drove us home and when we got there, Shane went to the shed while I got Ella out of the van. I gave Ella the key to the front door so I could go help Shane carry the Grill to the ramp. He rolled it up and I grabbed a little folding stand to set the plated hotdogs and Cheddar wursts next to the grill. It was a gas grill so it didn't take long to fire it up for cooking. He cooked up the meat while I set the table up in the dining room with the plates and glasses. I made some Country time lemonade in a pitcher, putting ice in to get it cold then set it in the middle of the table. Ella was watching some of the new She-Ra on Netflix and sitting on the floor. Shane finished cooking and brought the food in on a plate after just cooking for twenty minutes, setting it on the dining room table. I was surprised to see Shane walking so confidently with his one brace on. He made me proud to be near him since he was now recuperating from almost dying six months ago. Shane went over and started tickling Ella to distract her from the show.

"Time to eat little She-Ra," Shane said.

Shane picked up Ella like she was nothing and brought her over to her spot at the dining table then kissed her forehead. Shane sat down next to me as we ate the food, he prepared but then his phone started buzzing to life. Shane took a glance at his phone then turned to me.

"I better take this hon," Shane said.

"Ok," I replied.

He went to his now workout room and closed the door to talk while me and Ella finished our dinner up. Shane came back up with a smile on his face.

"I just got done talking to Evan and he says I can go get a free physical at a Gym in St. Paul and he has the paperwork for me Monday at Virgil's gym," Shane said.

"That's good love," I said.

I was now feeling a little panicky since it was now closer for him to fight, I just hoped he was getting back to his old self like he said. I knew that person could take care of anyone in the ring with his lightning speed fists. I was really unsure of Shane right now trying to get back in the ring. I knew I would have to try and watch him spar at the gym when it would start happening, to see how fast he was now. I could tell Shane could see my face looked worried since he grabbed my face with both hands and gave me a kiss.

"I will make sure I am totally ready before going back into the ring, hon," Shane said. "So, I won't get hurt ok."

"Alright, that's good to know," I said. "Don't forget in one more week we will have to drop off Ella at school before you train."

Shane smiled. "I can't wait to do that with you, Christine never let me do that with Tristan. Ella will you be glad being in second grade?"

"I can't wait to meet new people, papa," Ella replied.

It made me all giddy that he treated Ella like his own daughter as he touched her face then mussed up Ella's hair.

"I can't wait to take you to school," Shane said.

Shane finished eating while I did up the little dishes, we had then he came to the kitchen and did his own. I sat down next Ella and she laid her head on my shoulders while watching the live action movie, Sky High. Shane came and sat down next me on the couch, putting his arm around my shoulders. I leaned my head on his shoulder as we watched the movie, I felt so comfortable, I almost fell asleep. We watched Artemis Fowl next on Disney plus until it was over then we put Ella to bed. Shane told Ella a story about a knight that had to save a princess from a dragon. It was crazy how quick he could go into Dad mode; he was so good with Ella it was crazy. If I ever left this guy, I would slap myself upside the head, he definitely was the one type of guy I was looking for all my life. After he got done storytelling, Shane pulled the blanket over Ella then kissed her forehead. He grabbed my hand and led me back to the bedroom, where we made love until we were both spent. I laid in his arms and let him stroke my head as we lay in the darkness.

"When you start sparring, could I watch you at the gym?" I asked.

"I don't think Virgil would have a problem with it," Shane said. "It would be nice if you were there."

I turned my head slightly and smiled. "Thank you, Shane."

He kissed my forehead then hugged me in his arms tighter then let the tension go as we fell asleep. The next day came fast and Shane was working out in his room, where I woke up alone in bed. I got up then went and took a shower before going to wake up Ella to get her ready for the day. I was done dressing then went into Ella's room to shake her awake.

"Time to get up Ella, sleepy head," I said.

Her Elfin face lit up with a smile when she saw me. "Morning, Momma."

I pulled out some summer clothes for Ella from her dresser since it was supposed to be eighty degrees outside. I put a kid's tank top and shorts on the bed with the underwear, sock next to them.

"Don't forget you have to get a shower or a bath in tonight," I said.

"Yes, momma," Ella replied.

I went into the kitchen, scrambled eggs with bacon and made some toast to put in the middle of the dining room table. When the table was set, Shane came out wearing actual cargo shorts, white tank top, tennis shoes. His left calf muscle still seemed a little skinny but it looked healthier then when he first got out of the hospital. He came over and kissed me then sat down at the table with Ella.

"Good morning, little princess," Shane said, giving her a kiss on the forehead.

I sat down next to Shane and we began eating our breakfast then Shane spoke.

"Today, I need to go and pick up a speed bag and heavy bag for more training, if that's ok," Shane said.

"Sure, should we go after breakfast," I asked.

Shane nodded. "Yes, that would be fine and then we could take Ella to the Aquarium, down by the Bayfront Park."

I smiled. " Are you sure? That sounds like fun. Let's hurry and get done eating then, so we can get the show on the road."

We finished eating then Shane cleaned everything up while Ella and I got our shoes on to go to the store. We went to the mall at Dick's Sporting goods to pick up a life like male bust, heavy bag and a speed bag, that we loaded into the back of the van. We went back into the Miller hill mall and walked to the Build- a-bear workshop. Shane had them build a She-Ra bear; it was fun since Ella got to help build it then put the clothes on it. After it was all done, Ella hugged Shane then we continued walking around checking all the stores. We headed back to the van and drove back home to drop off the heavy bag and speed bag. I helped Shane to get the heavy bag into the house and in the workout room. It was on a stand so not so bad, just awkward then Shane went back to the van to get the speed bag. He came back with a power drill and I helped him put it at the right height, into the wall. Shane went to the kitchen and made cold cut sandwiches for us for lunch. He got some drinks and set it on the dining room table with the plate of sandwiches.

"Lunch is served, my dear ladies," Shane said.

Ella giggled then pulled herself away from the tv so she went to the table and I followed, since we watching some old, She-Ra that Shane picked up for her on DVD. We all sat down then Shane held out his hands for prayer.

"Dear Lord, I thank you for my new family and just ask for protection over us and the good times continue," Shane said.

I squeezed his hand then we dropped hands and began eating the sandwich for lunch, Ella was telling Shane about the show she was watching. Shane was nodding his head and laughing about the episode she talked about. I knew now God intended for me to save Shane just like he was giving his love for both of me and Ella. He was true husband and father, I intended when the time was right, I would ask for his hand in marriage.

"After lunch, lets hit the aquarium," Shane said.

"Ok," I said. "Sounds fun."

We drove down to the Bayfront aquarium and paid for the parking inside the lot before we headed into the building. While we were inside, Shane went into dad mode again and started talking about the different fishes. I held his hand as we walked around and checked the different stuff that was in the aquarium. It was a definitely a fun experience for me and Ella to go there, probably the most fun stuff she has done all year. Plus, the trip just getting to Duluth was a fun experience for her also. It was over an hour, before we finished going through the exhibit then we headed home. When we got home, we did our normal routine of getting some supper then something fun boardgame with

Ella. This time, Shane wanted her to learn how to play Monopoly. He must have had it in his old bedroom in the closet, where his father left it for him. We played it until I actually won by buying most of the properties and they kept landing on them, almost losing all their money. Shane and I put Ella to bed then we went back to our own bedroom, tearing our clothes off. We made love a long time then lay in the darkness, with my head resting on Shane's chest.

"Promise me, you won't fight until your as fast as you were before," I said.

"I promise you, Courtney, I will make sure I am truly ready before jumping into a fight," Shane said.

The rest of the weekend went by fast with Monday coming bright and early with Shane doing his normal run on the treadmill. I got some breakfast going, making eggs in basket with bacon and sausage. Shane must have taken a quick shower then dressed in his workout clothes and came out to eat breakfast Before he sat down, he mussed up Ella's hair, then began eating, he had one piece of toast to dip his egg with. This was Ella's last week before she would start the first grade and I knew Shane had to go down Wednesday for his physical.

"I have an idea since you have to take off an extra day of training for the physical," I said.

"What's your idea?" Shane asked.

"Since you have to go to ST. Paul for your physical," I said. "We could go to my sister's In Owatonna so you can meet her."

"Ok, it should only take a half hour then we could meet her somewhere," Shane said.

"Ok, I will set something up," I said.

We finished breakfast then Shane cleaned up the kitchen and table before we locked up the house. I unlocked the van and we all got in, buckling up then headed to the boxing gym.

Chapter Twenty-five

Shane

I was nervous after she asked me to meet her sister for some reason, maybe since Christine's parents ended up hating me after the accident, I suppose I didn't want someone saying I was taking advantage of Courtney in my vulnerable state. That would be a load of crap since she was actually more beautiful than Christine. Christine just kept her body in real good shape and took care of her hair. It was more like I fell in love with a natural beauty, just with a little bigger shape. Courtney was always going for walks with Ella at the park or the Lake walk while waiting for me get done training. I knew she didn't eat really bad at all and she always tried to keep her weight down so it never bothered me she had some bigger hips. We ended up at the gym about 9:30 AM, I jumped out of the van so I could unbuckle Ella from the booster seat. Courtney grabbed a coloring book, plus a book for her to read with the crayons. They both followed me into the boxing gym, where Virgil was standing by the counter with his hands behind his back. He had a slight smile on his face as he saw Courtney and Ella.

"Well, is this Mrs. Avis and your child, Mr. Avis?" Virgil asked.

"This is my girlfriend Courtney Ray and Cinderella Ray her daughter," I said. "They will be watching me train a little bit if that's ok."

I had looked at Courtney, who had a slight flush of red on her face after Virgil had asked if we were married.

"Well then, soon to be Mrs. Avis then, I have a good spot to sit so you can see all the action happening," Virgil said. "Follow me."

They followed Virgil while I went to the locker room to drop off my duffel bag and come back out to the gym. Virgil helped me put on my wraps then we got to work, where I hit the heavy bag for fifteen minutes. I switched to the speed bag for another twenty minutes, while Virgil set up the string across the boxing ring. I did the ducking underneath with uppercuts for another fifteen minutes where Virgil screamed at me to go faster. We got back into the boxing ring to work on focus mitts. Virgil pushed me hard for more speed and since Courtney was there, I guess, I was trying to impress her. Everything was about speed and I was definitely going to be tired after this workout session. He had pushed me harder on the heavy bag and speed bag also, screaming for me to go faster. Virgil pushed me over to the dumbbell rack and had me grab twenty-pound dumbbells to work with, he pushed me hard for almost ten minutes, I thought biceps were going to pop.

"Ten minutes, shadow boxing Mr. Avis, with speed then hit the showers," Virgil said.

Virgil headed over to Courtney and Ella talking to them while I did the shadow boxing in the mirror, building up speed. My arms felt like noodles after the ten minutes then I headed to the locker room and showered off. I changed into a different t-shirt and underwear and put my grey gym shorts back on. I headed out of the locker room and could see they were now standing by the front counter talking. I was going to the counter and Ella saw me, she ran to me to give me a hug around the waist. I kneeled down for a bit.

"Ella, were you ok being here for a bit with your mommy today?" I asked

"I can see why your getting better papa," Ella replied.

I smiled. "I am getting better now aren't I."

I stood back up and looked at Virgil. "What are we working on tomorrow?"

"We will work on your legs and balance tomorrow, Mr. Avis," Virgil said.

"Alright, have a good day, coach," I said.

I grabbed Ella's hand; Courtney gave a small wave to Virgil then we headed out the front door to the parking lot. Out in the parking lot, Evan Abrams was parked next to the van, holding a piece of paper in his hand. I helped Ella into the van then turned to shake Evan's hand as he handed me the paperwork.

"Thanks, for doing this Evan, I didn't expect any help from the old crew," I said.

"Hey, those dudes were A-holes anyways, all they cared about was getting money from you," Evan said. "It was a shit move to just leave you high and dry like that, with no explanation what so ever."

"In the car is Courtney, one of the nurses from the hospital, that has been helping me since I got out of the hospital and her daughter," I said.

Ella waved from the open van and Evan smiled and waved back.

"Nice to meet you," Evan called over my shoulder. "So, I see Vinny cut off his phone so no one can talk to him and I think Bell did too."

"Yeah, they must have thought I was never ever going to go back to boxing," I said.

"Your up and walking pretty good for thirty-six-year-old who almost died, I got faith you'll get back in the game and so does Virgil," Evan said.

"Thanks Evan, that means a lot to me, I suppose I better head out since it's getting warm in the van," I said as I closed the side door.

I shook his hand one more time than I got into the van and he got into his small Honda that was parked next to the van. We headed back home, and I looked over the sheet for the physical which was pretty standard to get a Pro license. The rest of the day went pretty fast and so did the next day. Courtney watched me again doing leg day this time but Virgil added more Shadow boxing after all the leg exercises, we did. Ella was coloring one of her books but watching once and in a while. I took my normal shower and changed into some other shorts and t-shirt before leaving the gym. We did a normal routine but I worked on filling out the information on the Physical paperwork while watching a movie. Once night came since I knew wasn't training, we made love again before bed. We woke up six in the morning, showered and dressed than got Ella ready to go for the trip to St. Paul.

I made sure I dressed summer clothing since it was pretty hot out. Tank top, cargo shorts, short socks, tennis shoes and baseball cap to cover the shaved head from the sun. Courtney put on a V-neck, grey t-shirt and grey cargo shorts with short socks and tennis shoes. I went to the fridge and got three bottles of water for us then I waited in the dining area. Ella looked sleepy but she was dressed in a t-shirt and shorts, had her sandals on. I picked her up while Courtney took the waters and I carried her to the van, to put her into the booster seat. I buckled her in and she closed her eyes, falling asleep in the seat and I kissed her forehead. I closed the side door and got into the passenger side, closing the door behind me as we drove away from the house.

Courtney stopped at the gas station and we filled up then got a breakfast sandwich so we could get back onto 35 south. It took us two hours to get down to St. Paul and another 25 minutes to find the gym, where they were having the physicals. I did get in after fifteen minutes of waiting in a line for the physical to getting it over with. They checked vitals and blood to make sure there was no HIV or nothing serious with each boxer that was getting a license. I brought the paperwork with me and signed a check for seventy dollars after all the testing. I got done then went to where there was a waiting room for families and got

Courtney, Ella out of there. I put coordinates in the GPS for Como Park Zoo so we could bring Ella there. I just hoped that Courtney would enjoy it too, for a field trip for Ella and us.

"Let's go here, hon," I said.

"Ok, Shane,' Courtney replied.

We drove to the zoo and found a parking space but still had to walk over a block to get to the front entrance. I stuck a twenty in the donation box before we went through the front entrance of the Zoo. We met her sister Lea and husband Jake at the Zoo so we could have Lunch and walk around with them. I felt we got along good, plus being at the Zoo with Ella made it easier. For the rest of the day, we followed the path in a big circle and checked out all of the animals that the zoo had to offer. We ate lunch in the big court yard they had and got pictures of the whole family by a zoo worker. All around it was a fun day and her sister was happy to meet me, it was late when we headed back home to Duluth. I got back to training the next day with a double ended speed ball, hitting it and dodging the ball with Virgil screaming for me to move faster. We worked on that for twenty minutes then headed to the heavy bag and speed bag. With both bags we worked another twenty minutes a piece then got into the ring. Virgil had me do the string, dodging and doing the uppercut for twenty minutes more. He brought out the focus mitts and we practiced with them for another twenty, dodging and hitting the mitts. I was sweating profusely once I got done so I hit the showers. I changed clothes and headed to the front counter, where Virgil sat talking to Courtney and Ella. I came up and then Virgil spoke to me.

"Tomorrow we actually start sparring again and work on foot movement inside the ring," Virgil said. "We need to see how your foot brace will hold up."

"You're moving up the sparring a week?" I asked.

"Yes, I have a young lightweight that is willing to help out,"

Virgil said. “I am training him for the Golden Gloves so you can give him some pointers as well.”

I smiled. “See you tomorrow coach.”

Virgil waved as we all left the building and we headed to the van to get in. I got Ella seated into the booster seat then got into the passenger side. We headed home to go do our usual routine for the night. I was wishing it was Friday so I could make love to Courtney but I just settled with cuddling her in the night. I woke up early again at seven AM to get my cardio running in, then I took a nice hot shower and dressed for the gym. I packed my usual change of shirt and underwear with a towel for my shower off at the gym. I went out to the dining room so I could have eggs and bacon with my new family. It was Memorial Day weekend so Ella would have to start 2nd grade at Lowell elementary. I never got to take Tristan since I was so caught up in the training or hanging with other boxing people that I missed it. This time I was going to go in with Ella and at least check on the teachers. We finished eating breakfast and I cleaned everything up while she got Ella in the Van. I locked the door behind me and jogged up to the van to get in, buckling my seat belt. We drove to the Lowell Elementary, where it was bustling with people so we got an end parking space near the front. I got her out of the seat and Ella was already wearing a long sleeved She-Ra shirt with, jeans, tennis shoes and carrying her backpack with school supplies. I took her hand after closing the side door and Courtney with her other hand, we brought Ella into the school. An older, heavier woman with her hair tied back, glasses, met us by her class, she wore a flowery dress.

“I am Della Peachtree, the second- grade teacher, this must be Cinderella Ray,” She smiled down at Ella.

“Yes, it is, Nice to meet you Della,” I said shaking her hand. “I'm Shane Avis.”

Courtney shook her hand. “I'm Courtney Ray, her mother.”

"Well, I hope your daughter enjoys being here or at least enjoys school," Della said.

I knelt by Ella and gave her a kiss on the forehead. "Try to behave Ella and make it through the day, little one, alright. Papa will have a gift for you after school."

"Ok, papa, "Ella said.

I smiled as she walked into the classroom and I got up then I took Courtney's hand and led her back to the van. We headed to the boxing gym and I was actually kind of nervous of trying to spar with someone, since I have not fought since the accident. It was nine thirty in the morning or a little after, once we got to the gym. Courtney followed me in with her book and I headed to the locker room to drop off my little duffel bag. I wrapped my hands inside the locker room so I was just ready for my workout with Virgil. I went out of the locker room to gym, where Virgil was standing next to the boxing ring. Next to Virgil, was a tall lanky young black man in a blue tank top and boxing shorts. He was pretty skinny but he was about 6 foot in height compared to my five foot six inches. He was in the golden gloves standard fighting outfit that was used in all of those matches, with long arms. He had a big reach so this would be an interesting sparring match between us. I went over to both of them to greet them as he put some gloves on the kid.

"Hey coach, how's it going?" I asked.

Virgil smiled. "Mr. Avis, this is my grandson, Demetrius Steward. You will be sparring him at least twice a week. The purpose will be to avoid the blows, getting your head movement at full speed so in a real fight, you'll be able to take care of business."

I nodded then touched gloves with Demetrius. "It's good to meet you kid. I hope we learn from each other."

Virgil made sure my gloves were on tight before letting both of us, to get into the boxing ring as Virgil prepared to hit the bell.

Chapter Twenty-six

Courtney

I was sitting in a chair, near the boxing ring, chewing on my fingernails as I watched Shane begin to spar with the tall skinny black kid. I was really worried about Shane getting hurt since I didn't know how good he was now after the rehab. They began to move around the ring, while Virgil yelled at them to start throwing punches. Shane seemed confident as he moved his head like a whip lash from Demetrius's punches. He began peppering the kid with lightning-fast jabs as Virgil would be screaming good then faster. By round five, Shane was tired and getting hit by Demetrius but still getting his jabs and roundhouse punches in. While round five was going, Virgil had to take a call on his cellphone. Virgil's face lit up as he hit the bell and he cut his phone call, putting the cellphone back in his pocket. He helped Shane and Demetrius out of the boxing ring by holding the rope for them.

"That was a good sparring session guys," Virgil said. "Shane, I got some good news, you have a fight scheduled at the Armory, at the end of September, against Huey Baxter, Lightweight division."

Shane smiled. "That's great coach! I can't wait for the fight."

"You will probably end up with 2500 after all the payments," Virgil said. "I have to take my cut and Evan will get some also."

"That's fine coach, I just want to fight again," Shane said.

I helped take off Shane's gloves then handed him a towel to wipe the sweat off his face, while Virgil helped his grandson get his gloves off.

“Your boxing license should show up before then Mr. Avis and we can get down to business,” Virgil said. “We will continue with a five round sparring session, once a week.”

“Alright, sounds good coach. I’m going to hit the shower,” Shane said.

Shane went to the lockers, while I found a chair near the front desk, that Virgil sat at, when he was waiting for customers to come in. I sat in the chair, while Virgil came back to the front desk to sort through his mail that was dropped off earlier. I decided to ask him the question, if Shane was ready to fight yet.

‘Virgil, do you think Shane is ready to fight in the pros again?” I asked.

Virgil looked at me and smiled. “I believe so, Mrs. future Avis. The fights that are coming up are low caliber pro fights. I would worry if it was a championship fight and that won’t happen for almost a year.”

I nodded. “It’s good to know. I really don’t want to see Shane hurt bad. He looks almost like himself from the old fights but the left foot slows him down.”

“That’s where the heads movement comes in so he can dodge blows and use his punching power to knock out the opponents,” Virgil said.

Shane came out of the locker room, wearing jeans and a He-Man t-shirt, tennis shoes. He came over to the front desk and I stood up to leave.

“See you Monday coach,” Shane said.

“Have a good weekend, Mr. and Mrs. Avis,” Virgil said.

We left the boxing gym and headed home since we still had a couple of hours to ourself before picking up Ella. Shane made us a healthy sub sandwich for lunch and set some chips on the plates with bottled water. It was tasty with mayo and some ranch on the sub, turkey slices, lettuce, tomatoes topped it. Recently, it seemed like Shane wanted more healthy food for supper so I made sure every dinner had vegetables and no heavy carbs with the meat. Shane now actually weighed 135 pounds now so he looked ripped and healthy as a boxer. Once we finished eating, Shane led me to the bedroom and took off my clothes, making passionate love. I laid cuddled up in bed with Shane as he stroked my hair and then he popped the question.

"Win or lose my next fight, I would like to marry you Courtney, "Shane said. "With your permission of course. Also, I would like to have my lawyer get paperwork to adopt Ella."

I was shocked and almost speechless, when Shane said that, I knew I wanted to be with Shane for the rest of my life but marriage scared me for some reason. Probably since I was married to Travis and it ended up him getting dead from his drugs, gambling addiction that it gave me pause.

"If you promise to never let yourself hide any problems we are having, I will say yes to marrying you Shane," I said.

"I promise and understand your concerns, Courtney. I will always treat you like a queen and take care of Ella as my own daughter," Shane said.

I looked up at Shane then pushed my head forward, so I could kiss his lips and my head be cradled by Shane with a long kiss. After that, I looked up at the clock to check the time and saw it read, 1:30 PM, both Shane and I got dressed. Shane beat me as he finished tying his tennis shoes and went out to the kitchen to grab two pizzas from the freezer. I came out of the bedroom, after I put my own shoes on. I headed to the kitchen where Shane put both pizzas into the oven for baking.

"Go ahead and get Ella, while I cook and get the table set up for early dinner," Shane said.

"Alright, babe," I said.

I picked up my keys from a hook, next to the front door and headed out to the van to go start it up. I headed to the Lowell School to get to the pick-up spot, so I could get Ella from the school grounds. Ella was waiting at a corner with her back pack on so I parked next to her and got out, getting her into her seat. I closed the side door then got back into the driver seat so we could get back on the road towards home.

"How was your day at school, Ella?" I asked.

"The math was pretty hard today since it was multiplication but overall, it ok," Ella said.

"Well, I can try to help you alright, Shane is making an early supper so later we can have ice cream," I said.

The rest of the ride, Ella was silent, looking out the window as I drove us back to the house, the traffic was a little slow today. I parked in the driveway then got out so I could get Ella out of the van. I went to unbuckle her and she gave me a hug and I gave her a kiss on the cheek then finished unbuckling her. Ella went sprinting towards the house as I closed the van doors and followed her in. I closed the door behind me then saw Shane in the kitchen putting some paperwork in a manila envelope as Ella grabbed his waist and hugged him.

"How was school little She-Ra?" Shane asked.

"It was fine, I missed you guys," Ella said.

"We missed you too, Ella," Shane said and kissed her forehead.

The table was all set up with plates, plastic cups and a pitcher of lemonade sat on the table also as Shane grabbed the pizza out of the oven. He set hot pads down then took a pizza cutter and cut the pizza into triangles.

"I have one more pepperoni and sausage pizza in the oven," Shane said.

"Very nice dear," I said and enjoyed saying that.

Ella went to her room to put her backpack away then I and Shane sat down at the table next to each other while we waited for her. She came in the kitchen and sat opposite of us then we prayed before eating. The first pizza disappeared quickly after our prayer, then we put the pizzas on our plates to take to the living room. We watched some shows for a little bit together than Shane went to work out in his exercise room. I had Ella turn off the tv then we worked on a She-Ra puzzle I picked up from Amazon. It took us a couple of hours to complete the puzzle, while Shane finished working out and showering. The night ended and I read a story for Ella before her bedtime. Shane came in and gave Ella a kiss on the forehead then we went to our room to go to sleep.

The next week flew by for me and Shane as training for the first boxing match. Shane surprised me with a decent sized ring for my finger and showed me the paperwork for the adoption for Ella. He still had to wait until we were officially married, which we agreed on a court marriage. I drove all of us down to the Armory for the fight with Huey Baxter, Virgil included. Evan was already at the Armory when Shane went to get dressed for his fist fight in a year. Ella and I sat in the front row with the roaring crowd behind us and could see Virgil double checking Shane's gloves. He was standing as he spoke to Evan and Virgil as the gloves, even nut cup checked before they went to the middle of the ring. The ring announcer stood in the middle, holding a microphone to his mouth.

"In this corner! former number one contender in the middle weights, twenty-five KO's and zero losses, Shane "Lightning Fists" Avis!!!," the ring announcer roared, pointing in Shane's direction.

The ring announcer then spun around and pointed at Huey. "In this corner! Huey Baxter! Ten wins and one loss. Let's get ready to rumble!!!!"

I was feeling really nervous as Shane went to the middle with his crew to see the ref, Huey was a little skinnier white guy. He wore red and black trimmed trunks, while Shane wore black trunks with a white lightning stripe on the side. The referee said a few things then they touched gloves then went back to their corners to await the bell. I took Ella's hand as the bell rang and they moved to the middle to begin feeling each other out.

"Papa, will be ok momma," Ella said.

I smiled at her. "I think your right Ella."

Shane was moving around the ring slow but using his head to dodge punches and his gloves to block some of them also. It was about two minutes into the fight then Shane unloaded on Huey with a flurry of blows that knocked him down hard. The crowd got up and began cheering for Shane as they counted Huey Baxter out. Shane turned and practically lifted Virgil off the ground in excitement. It was his first big win in over a year, Shane proved to everyone even he was crippled he could win again in the ring. Shane lived up to his promise, in the coming weeks, we got married at the Duluth Court house, in October. He had a friend from high school as his best man, Bill Edgards and both our parents showed since it was not winter yet. My sister, Edie was my maid of honor. It was an exciting day and to top it off, once we got home, we were able to show Ella her official adoption papers. Ella cried with joy once we told her the good news and hugged both of us. We were now officially the Avis family and it felt good that God gave us a second chance for both of us.

Shane actually fought twice more at the Armory and gave him two more knockouts, that made him undefeated in the Lightweight division. He was training for his fourth fight, that was supposed to be in Hinkley Grand Casino. I was riding an exercise bike while Shane and Virgil worked on his shadow boxing with five-pound dumbbells. The phone began to ring at the front counter so Virgil stopped to go answer. Shane stopped and took a drink from a water bottle as Virgil took his call.

Chapter Twenty-seven

Shane

I was taking a swig of my water bottle in the ring and drying the sweat off my face as Virgil took his phone call. Virgil finished talking and hung up old black dial phone then headed back into the boxing ring.

"Well, Mr. Avis. After this fight, if you win, you have an offer for a championship fight," Virgil said. "You will have a chance to fight Juan Ortiz, in Las Vegas, Nevada."

"That's great! I can have my folks show up for the fight," I said. "They give you an amount I would make for the fight?"

"Mr. Avis, if you were to win it would be two million dollars," Virgil said. "If you were to lose five hundred thousand. Just remember you have some expenses for the crew."

"That doesn't worry me, was just wondering coach," I said. "Let's get back to work."

We finished the work out and I was psyched for the next fight with Avery Holmes, a black fighter, who was tough. He had a very good record, twenty wins with one loss, at least thirteen KO's. Virgil pushed the speed up in every workout and that included sparring with Demetrius since he was close to winning the Golden Glove Championship himself. Before the big boxing match at the Casino, I went with Courtney to watch Demetrius's fight in the Golden Gloves. It was an exciting match since Demetrius was lightning fast with his punches like me. Ella sat on my left side, and I had my arm around her shoulder while watching the fight. I held Courtney's hand as the action got intense. Demetrius knocked out his opponent in the third last round of the fight. I stood up with the rest of the people as we cheered for his win. Virgil was in his corner for this fight so it was exciting to see.

The next following week, was my fight at the Hinkley Grand Casino with Virgil and Evan. Demetrius wanted to be part of the crew so he also was in my corner. There was a decent crowd at the casino for the fight and that made me psyched. This fight did not take that long at all, once I got Avery backed up on the ropes. I let loose with a flurry of blows and an uppercut that put Avery on his ass. The ref started the count and Avery just looked dazed trying to get back up. He couldn't and the crowd went wild as I raised my hands in victory, it was an exciting feeling to know I was a championship contender again. When I got home, I called my father to let him know the good news, he answered on the second ring.

"How's it going kiddo?" Don asked.

"I just got a championship fight, against Juan Ortiz in the Lightweight division," I said. "It will be held in Las Vegas."

"That's great! I will let your mother know. How long before your manager sets it up?" Don asked.

"I'm sure by next week he will be working on the details of the fight and negotiating the price of the fight," I said.

"Well, try to get the most money you can," Don said. "I know now at least you're living more economically than before. No flashy cars or mansion. You can't box forever Shane."

"I know dad, I will be opening my own gym in a year," I said. "Probably in Vegas since Courtney's parents and sister live there now."

"Good idea to have a back up plan, alright I will let your mother know," Don said. "Have a good night, Shane."

I hung up the phone then change into pajamas so I could relax some, while Courtney got ice cream in bowls for us. We sat down and watched an episode of He-man with Ella; I got her hooked since She-Ra always shows up sometimes. After the episode, Courtney put Ella to bed and we went to our bedroom and made love. In the mornings, when Courtney made breakfast, I would pray after I did a three-mile run on the treadmill. God gave me a second chance and I always prayed for protection for my new family. The next few weeks of training went by and Virgil had set up the fight. It would take place in March, so I had two months to train before the match. Virgil upped the sparring with Demetrius and wanted me to work more on dodging, blocking punches for my training. I would do laps in the morning, around the mall since the walks were clear from snow. I would do that twice a week, with my 3 miles on the treadmill and lots of stretching. My left foot was really good now without the brace, less flopping on me and more strength in the ankle.

Virgil had one day of legwork with doing heavy squats, calf raises, walking lunges, deadlifts, it really improved the weak left foot. He made me do a ton of pushups and sit-ups but not a lot of benches pressing. He also cut the arm work down so I wouldn't go over the muscle mass weight and get over the lightweight title. I even got my jump roping perfected with the floppy left foot. I ate a lot of Subway wraps and salads or vegetable soups to keep the weight down at 135 pounds. I was definitely ripped for the fight and my hands now had the lightning speed it had before the accident. I set up the flight to Vegas for Courtney, Ella and I before the weekend. We would have to pull Ella from school for a few days, but it would be worth it since I got a room with the Excalibur hotel. Both Evan and Virgil, got a room somewhere else cheaper and would just meet at the MGM Grand. It would be where the fight would be held with Juan Ortiz.

We took a flight from Duluth on a Thursday to Vegas to get settled into the hotel room and have some fun at the hotel. I had to go over to the MGM Grand and meet up with Virgil, Evan for the weigh in and conference right away. I weighed in exactly at

135 pounds for the match, so did Juan Ortiz, who looked like a monster at 135. I didn't say too much, just that I was glad God gave me a second chance to try and become a champion and wished Juan good luck. I got back to the hotel and went with Ella and Courtney to dinner at the Excalibur with Jousting. We watched the jousting matches that they had there while we ate a nice supper. Ella enjoyed every minute of the jousting and giggled at the knights who got knocked down from their horses. I made sure we went to bed by nine at night since I knew I had jetlag from the trip. Virgil got into Vegas and actually got a room with Evan at the MGM Grand for the night. The fight was scheduled at nine that night against Ortiz, the crowd would be huge since there was one other championship fight that night. The other fight was light heavy weight champ, Darius 'Sweet Daddy' Williams, defending his title against Damien Bell. I did not look forward to even glancing at him since Darius, nor Vinny contacted me after the hospital. I must have looked bothered by it in the morning since Courtney said something.

"You alright Shane?" Courtney asked.

I looked over at her. "Yeah, just hoping I don't see Vinny or Darius since both of them just left me high and dry."

I finished dressing so we could meet up with Courtney's parents for breakfast then we were supposed to meet my parents for lunch. Both events went well and we had fun with Ella along with us. It was a warm day since it was in march, at seventy degrees already, a lot warmer than Duluth was when we left. I was dressed in jeans and a V neck pocket T-shirt that was light blue, with tennis shoes. It was ironic, Courtney wore a grey v - neck shirt and Ella a white V- neck t-shirt so we pretty much matched. I only ate a little bit for both breakfast and lunch so dinner was just a sub wrap from Subway. I got my duffel bag ready then we caught a shuttle over to the MGM Grand. It was full of people walking around, probably because the all fights started at seven thirty at night. It was now five O'clock so I was glad we got there to try and find the locker room I was supposed to be in. I found a security guard and got directions to get to the locker room from where we were at. That's when I bumped into my old coach Vinny as I almost got to it.

"Hey kid, looking good there," Vinny said. "When do you want to come back to the big leagues?"

"I have a good manager and trainer Vinny," I said. "He's big enough for me and hasn't left me high and dry."

"Kid, I do want to apologize for that," Vinny said. "Darius wanted to move to Vegas so I decided to go with him. I thought you would be with your folks for awhile so I could get a hold of you."

"Vinny, I forgive you but our business is done," I said. "Good luck with you and Darius."

I took off to the locker room before Vinny could get another word in edgewise, opening the door heading in. I could see Demetrius in a promotion shirt for me, with Virgil pacing back and forth, Evan sitting on a bench. Virgil's face lit up with a smile.

"Mr. Avis, right on time," Virgil said. "Ready to get dressed and hands taped up."

I set my bag down. "I'm ready to become a champion coach."

Both Courtney and Ella went to go find their seats as I got my black and white lightning striped boxing trunks on. I made sure the nut cup was adjusted right so it wouldn't bug me through the fight. Virgil taped up my hands as I focused thinking about the run in with Vinny, a man that was just worried about money. Virgil must have noticed my far-off look.

"You alright Mr. Avis?" Virgil asked.

"I ran into Vinny as I was trying to find the locker," I said. "I'm just bugged by it a little."

"I now how you feel, I was once let go by my manager and trainer when I fell in some hard times," Virgil said. "All we can do is forgive and forget. Try to focus on this match, Shane so you can win this since you poured all of this hard work to getting here."

I was surprised when he said my first name." Thanks coach, your right."

Virgil finished with my hand wraps then I began on doing some leg and arm stretches to get my muscles loosened up. I began shadow boxing next to a mirror to get a good sweat started, with the muscles loosening. The time flew by since the first championship match started at 7:30 pm with Darius defending his title. I only caught glimpses of the match on the tv in the locker room while Virgil talked strategy with me for my match. Darius knocked out his opponent in the fourth round and kept his belt. About nine pm, a Security knocked on the door and said they were ready for our entrance. I just put a towel on my shoulders like Mike Tyson does, instead of wearing a robe, easier to take off. Virgil put my gloves on and taped them on before we began walking down the tunnel to the boxing ring. I had the people from the MGM Grand put the song 'Eye of the Tiger' by survivor as my entrance song. I stepped out of the tunnel with my crew behind me and Virgil's hand on my shoulder. The song blared, with the roar of the crowd surrounding me as we headed to the ring. I had gotten my folks and my new family seats right next to my corner so they could see me. I gave small wave to them as I entered the ring with my crew.

I could see on the other side of the ring was Juan 'The Beast' Ortiz, who looked like a beast for being a lightweight. I could tell he was going to give me the challenge of my life, once the bell rang for us. The ring announcer, who looked like Michael Buffer in his tuxedo, grabbed a microphone that has lowered in front of him. He pointed at me first.

"In this corner! Former middle weight contender, Shane 'Lightning Fists' Avis! A record of twenty-six ko's and zero losses!!!," The ring announcer yelled then whipped around to the other side of the ring.

“In this corner!! Is the lightweight champion of the world! Juan ’The Beast’ Ortiz!!! Forty wins and 3 losses! “The ring announcer yelled.” Let’s get ready to rumble!!!”

The referee signaled for us to move in the middle of the ring and we moved forward to meet Ortiz at the middle.

“Let’s have a clean fight with no low blows or cheap shots, got it,” The ref said. “let’s touch gloves.”

I nodded and touched his gloves then went back to my corner, where Virgil squirted water on my face then wiped it quick.

“Alright, let’s stick to what we trained,” Virgil said. “Stick and move, feel him out the first round, get to it.”

The Bell sounded almost like a church gong as it went off and I began to move around the ring to memorize his moves. Juan was known for trying to get the knockout in the first round so he was on the move to try and take off my head. I was glad I had trained in the head movement and blocking or I might have been knocked out. By the end of the first round, I was able to get some good shots in. Evan checked my face then cleaned it and put the mouth piece in while Virgil talked.

“Great first round, now start getting some jabs in to punish him,” Virgil said.

“Ok, coach,” I said then he stuck in the mouth piece.

The next two rounds were brutal, as we traded blows and gave facial cuts to each other, my ears were ringing. Juan got lucky and caught my ear in a punch so all I could hear was ringing and none of Virgil’s advice. The fourth round we were trading blows and he caught me up against the ropes. I was trying to rope a dope as much as I could from the punches but I got caught with a good uppercut then a few other hard punches the pushed me to the mat. I was in a slight daze as the ref began counting and I began struggling to stand. I could hear Virgil screaming and my father yelling for me to get up. Everything felt like it was in slow motion for me, but that's when I thought I had heard Tristan call to me.

"Papa, it's time to get up, please papa," Tristan's voice called out.

I could see tears in Ella's eyes as I struggled to get up and she screamed for me to get up. I pushed myself up by nine and the bell rang. Virgil got me on the stool and Evan went to work on my cuts on the face.

"Mr. Avis, you gave me a big scare there," Virgil said. "Start sticking and moving until you get some wind back got it. You can do this Shane; you can become champion if you tire this guy out"

I nodded as he stuck the mouthpiece back in. "Got it coach."

The next round, I worked on moving and hitting Juan with a jab to his right eye, that was already damaged. I could see in the fifth round, that Juan was beginning to run out of gas, his punches were lagging. By the seventh round, I found an opening and cornered Juan in the ropes with my own flurry of blows. The crowd was going wild since this was a back-and-forth fight from the beginning between to gladiators not giving up. I gave Juan two hard uppercuts to the head then he bounced off the ropes, falling to the mat. Juan had gone flat on his face as the ref began his count to ten. I ran back to my corner as he counted and I could see Juan actually looked like he was knocked out. The ref waved his arms for the end of the fight and I fell to my knees, laughing, crying in joy. The crew lifted me up and I could hear the crowd going wild when they called the fight. I felt kind of worried when the doctor ran over to Juan with his crew to try and revive him. They were able to, and I felt relief so I ran over to tell him I was sorry, making sure he wasn't going to be permanently damaged from the blows I gave him. I went back to my corner than they told us to go to the middle for the announcement. The ring announcer grabbed the microphone then looked to the judges.

"By a seventh-round knockout, your new champion! Shane 'Lightning fists' Avis!!!!" The ring announcer spoke loudly as he handed me the belt.

The roar of the crowd was incredible as I raised my championship belt in the air for everyone to see. I put it on my shoulders then a tv reporter came to ask some questions.

"That was an impressive wine, Shane," The male reporter said. "I could tell after the fourth-round close call you changed your game plan and came out victorious. How do you feel?"

"I just want to thank God for my second chance at life and my trainer Virgil for a second chance to become a champion. My new family has given me the strength to make a come back and I dedicate this fight for Courtney and Ella," I said. "I wouldn't be here today because of them, God bless."

I turned away from the reporter as he finished talking to the camera while I headed straight back to the locker room with the crew. We headed back to Duluth, Minnesota the next day on a flight at one pm. When we got back, I did what I told my dad I was going to do and only fought two more times than retired. I was truly blessed when the adoption went through and Ella became my daughter. I bought a gym in Las Vegas with a boxing ring but lot of exercise equipment so ordinary people could workout. My father was happy that I built a gym there so we could at least hang out more. We golfed and bowled a lot together as a family. Plus, Courtney was able to see her parents again since they had moved from Iowa to a retirement community in Las Vegas to try and get close to her. I was truly blessed to be alive and with my family again. I knew I had survived the knockout of almost dying then the knockout in the ring, God had been very gracious with me. I planned on not squandering the time I had on earth just working but being with my family and being happy.

The End

Made in the USA
Monee, IL
05 February 2024

52048770R10098